Pen to Page

Burnavon Writers

arts & culture
COOKSTOWN DISTRICT COUNCIL

GoodRelations
COOKSTOWN DISTRICT COUNCIL

Published by Arts & Cultural Development, Cookstown District Council

Cover illustration by George Gourley

© 2010 Burnavon Writers & Arts & Cultural Development, Cookstown District Council

ISBN   978-0-9565586-0-2

Foreword

As Chairman of Cookstown District Council's Arts and Cultural Sub Committee, I am delighted that the work of many talented writers has finally made its way into print.

The Burnavon Writers Group has gone from strength to strength since its inception in April 2008 as part of Cookstown District Council's Arts and Cultural Development programme and I congratulate all the contributors. They have much to be proud of. The variety and quality of their writing is most impressive and there is, within the following pages, something for everyone.

Members of the group, who are from within the district and beyond, are made up of those who previously attended creative writing classes and others who share an interest in creative writing. They have been meeting fortnightly at the South West College and have benefited from the tuition of Damian Gorman as well as ongoing guidance and support from Maura Johnston. A sincere thank you to both. I would also like to acknowledge the work of the Council's Arts and Cultural Officer, Mary Crooks, in facilitating this project.

Finding time to pursue our interests and talents can be difficult but, as "Pen to Page" shows, perseverance brings fulfilment and a feeling of achievement in what has been accomplished.

To the members of the Burnavon Writers Group I wish you continued success and, to those who are about to read what they have written, thank you for your support and enjoy!

Councillor Trevor Wilson
Chairman, Arts & Cultural Sub Committee, Cookstown District Council

Introduction

Writing to one's satisfaction is not an easy thing. Whether it is groaning over a blank sheet in the privacy of your home or biting nails with the frustration of not being able to think of the exact word or trying to beat the clock in a writing group – the pressure is on.

But pressure or no, belonging to a writers group brings its own rewards. First of all there is the discipline of writing to a theme, or in a particular form, and doing this within a specified time frame. Then there is the delight of learning something about one's own capabilities and the pleasure of articulating exactly a thought or feeling. Perhaps the best things are the sharing with like-minded souls and the encouragement that is at the heart of such a group.

A writers' group can help improve the craft of writing, but the soul of a work comes from the writers themselves. The members of Burnavon Writers Group have nurtured the spark within them. They have shared, struggled, laughed and encouraged one another. They have profited from the interaction. They have enjoyed themselves. And, importantly, they have persevered with their writing.

The writing in this book is varied. There are short stories, poems, essays, reminiscences, character portraits. There is pathos, excitement and humour. There is, as one would expect, a variety of styles.

Some of the authors are writers with years of experience; others are novices of the art. But the standard of writing is high and I think you will find there is something for everyone to enjoy.

Maura Johnston

Contents

Des Chada

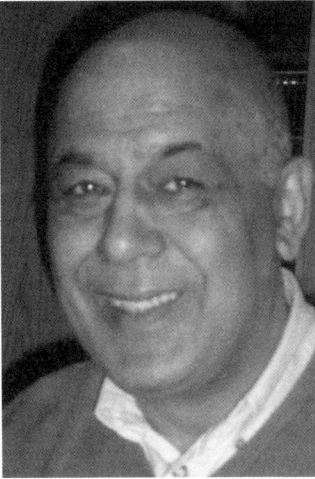

Des is married to Sue and they have two grown up children, one living in Manchester and the other in Hong Kong. He works for the Roads Service in the local section office in Magherafelt, dealing with a variety of maintenance issues. In his spare time he enjoys watching sport, reading and eating out with family and friends.

About two years ago he saw the advertisement promoting a writers class in Cookstown and thought, 'Why not?' Although he didn't have an arts background, he always felt that it was something that he wanted to try. Having been a member now for two years he can say he has no regrets. He finds that the common interest in this group can help people to connect and encourage friendships to develop beyond the group setting.

The Big School

"Good morning children."

"Good morning Sir," we replied in perfect unison.

It was our first day at the 'big school' and all the preliminary details had been sorted in the morning when timetables had been issued, term time rules had been explained and, most importantly, the geography of the school had been photocopied and given to every one of the new arrivals, many of whom had come from a school where there were possibly only three or four classrooms in total. Apparently there were eighty four boys and girls altogether, all dressed in the regulation grey and white uniform, with a red and black school tie to distinguish us from other schools. I had made my way to Room 10, along with Tubby Thompson and Duck Dinsmore, who had made the transition with me from our old primary school. We hadn't been particularly friendly before but they were the only ones in the French class that I knew, and even at the tender age of eleven, I knew that new alliances had to be made.

"My name is Mr Johnston, and you will call me Monsieur Johnston when you address me in class. Is that understood?"

"Yes Monsieur Johnston," came the uniform reply, as if we had been secretly practising speaking in one voice.

"Right, do any of you know any French words?" he asked.

Two of the class confidently put up their hands. I raised mine partially while the remainder remained nervously motionless.

"You there boy, what's your name?" he asked, pointing at a geeky looking individual in the front row.

"Peter Simpson," he answered.

"What's your word?"

"Croissant, Monsieur Johnston."

"And do you know what it means?"

"It's a type of bread."

"Very good," said Mr Johnston, causing Simpson to beam from ear to ear, as if he had just gained first place in a French exam.

"And you, young lady, what's your name and word?"

"My name is Lucy Chambers, and my word is RSVP."

"And the meaning is?" asked Mr Johnston.

"Well Sir, it means reply soon via post," she answered.

"Not exactly, but it's close enough," he replied.

"And you boy, what French words do you know," pointing in my general question.

"Grand pricks," I responded in a whisper.

"What's that boy, louder," he demanded.

"Grand pricks," I shouted, as the class erupted in loud and unsympathetic laughter. I'm not convinced that most of them even knew what they were laughing at, but were simply behaving in a herd instinct. When one laughed, they all laughed. Although I had read the words numerous times, I had never actually heard them spoken, and it was only after Mr Johnston gained his own composure that he explained that 'grand prix' was not pronounced as 'grand pricks'. My first class in the big school had resulted in the most humiliating few minutes of my life so far, so the bell for the end of class was a welcome diversion.

I groped in my blazer pocket to study the already crumpled timetable and subsequently made my way to Room 30 where I joined the rest of the class. I looked around for a familiar face and rapidly realised that there didn't appear to be any boys in the group.

"What's going on?" I thought, as I took a seat at the back of the room, "and why is everyone looking at me?"

The teacher, Mrs Dickson, made herself known to everyone, and then immediately focused on me.

"I think it's really beneficial for boys to know how to cook and look after a home," she said, with a smirk on her face, "but you're the first boy to enrol in our Domestic Science class since I've taught at the school."
How was I to know that 'Domestic Science' meant cooking? I assumed that the word science related to physics and chemistry, and had nothing to do with baking buns or creating casseroles. I seemed to be lurching from one crisis to another, and for the second time in a day I had a classroom of pupils laughing at me.

Last two periods were PE, and being a natural athlete, I soon gained the admiration of all the other boys as we played basketball in the gym and I managed to score more points than the rest of our team put together. I quickly put my earlier mishaps out of my mind and enjoyed being the centre of attention for more positive reasons, rather than being an object of ridicule.

The end of the class came and everyone rushed downstairs to the changing rooms, but Mr McConkey, the PE teacher, delayed me for a few moments while he complimented me on my basketball skills. I then rushed down the stairs and into the changing room where I was greeted with a chorus of screams, as twenty girls attempted to cover their nakedness. In a flash I realised that two hands weren't enough to cover the bits that were of interest to me, and some of the more developed girls had to make choices. Fortunately, for me anyway, they all managed to leave something for my hungry eyes to feast on. It was heaven and hell all at once, although I hadn't anticipated a biology class during PE. As I made a hasty retreat, although not too hasty, I realised that I should have turned left at the bottom of the stairs, and not right. This little adventure soon became the talk of the first form and before long I had manipulated the story so that the rest of the boys believed that I had gone into the girl's changing rooms deliberately.

Hero status was something that I easily adapted to as I was befriended, and then interrogated by practically every male in junior school. Any fears I may have had about not fitting in, or making new friends had become redundant, as news of the incident quickly spread. It became virtually impossible for me to walk in the corridor without the boys greeting me like a life long friend, while the girls acknowledged me coyly, then giggled. Life in the big school looked as if it was going to be sweet.

The Troubles

As I slowly made my way into the house the atmosphere transformed from peaceful mourning into tangible hatred. Each of the relatives or friends that were in attendance ensured that I was in no doubt that I was not welcome there. I jostled my way through the narrow corridor into the living room and wished that I was someplace else, but this was something that I had to do. After all, Tariq and I had been friends from birth, literally. Our mothers had met in the local hospital during the latter stages of their pregnancy and become friends, and when the time came to make our appearance in this world we arrived within hours of each other. After the midwife delivered him she moved to the adjacent bed and started on me. Although he was the elder by only three hours he took his seniority seriously and for the fourteen years that he lived, he always looked after me, and often had the bruises to show for it. Tariq was as much a part of my family as I was of his, and consequently rarely a day went by without some contact between us.

His family home was in the predominantly Muslim quarter, while I lived in the Hindu part of town. This had never been a significant problem before but now that India was on the verge of gaining independence from British rule, tensions had been mounting between the two religious factions, and there were demands that Muslims should be given their own country. This idea was not favoured by the vast majority of the country but it was being given serious consideration by the British parliament. They knew that their days were numbered on the sub continent and a speedy withdrawal was their main aim. Riots started to break out and before long, Muslims were not safe in Hindu areas, and Hindus were not safe in Muslim areas. It was on the journey home from my house that Tariq was confronted by a mob seeking some sort of revenge. It appeared that he tried to escape but he was heavily outnumbered, and never stood a chance. Insanity prevailed and he was butchered by people who had previously watched him grow up. My own neighbours had decided that a fourteen year old boy was a threat to their future. Within minutes he was no more.

His mother looked up as I entered the room. Twenty four hours of tears were etched on her face. She had lost her elder son and I felt as if I was responsible. I wanted to cry out that it wasn't my fault but I couldn't speak. Instead a torrent of grief gushed from my eyes as she held out her arms to comfort me and I wept like never before. Tariq was buried the following day and over the following few weeks many thousands of other innocents were massacred in the name of religion.

My family left India shortly afterwards, believing that the violence would only get worse, and that it was not a suitable place to bring up a family. My father had friends in Northern Ireland who suggested that it was an ideal place to start a business and raise the family. Decisions were made quickly and within a few months we had embarked on the long boat journey to Southampton. A second, but shorter, sea crossing landed us in Belfast which I have called home for the past thirty years.

Settling in Ireland was made easy for us, due mainly to the friendly nature of the indigenous population, but also because of the work ethic that we had. Most had never seen an Indian before and often I had to explain that I had never been in dispute with any cowboys. That often disappointed my school friends who wanted to hear stories about Jesse James or General Custer.

Thirty years passed, and one night, in my broad Belfast accent, I answered a phone call at home when I was informed that my friend Imran had been killed. He was Tariq's younger brother and had been staying with me for the past month while he looked for a job. He had gone into town earlier that day for an interview at a computer software company, with high hopes of securing a job with them. Not only had he gained an Honours degree in computer programming, but he had spent a number of years heading a team in a major software firm in Delhi, skills that made him an ideal candidate for the job. Apparently the interview went very well and he was offered the job immediately. His jubilation prompted him to stop for a drink on his way home but he never got to finish it. A car bomb exploded outside the pub in the predominantly loyalist area, killing four people and injuring seventeen. This was in retaliation to the bomb placed the previous night on the Falls Road, and simply continued the tit for tat bombings that were a feature of the current conflict.

I travelled back to India for the funeral, and once again made my way down the same narrow corridor into the living room where Imran's mother received the many mourners. Again, I felt partially responsible for her son's death since he was in my charge when the murder took place, but in my heart I knew that fanatics, three thousand miles apart, had taken her two sons and left her childless, all because of religious intolerance. I moved towards her in response to her open arms and for the second time we comforted each other. I realised that Gandhi's words, spoken in India thirty years earlier were just as applicable now in Belfast, when he said, "An eye for an eye just leaves the world blind."

Decisions Decisions

It was precisely six thirty when the digital clock radio started to broadcast the sounds of Radio London. Roberto stirred, then stretched, and forced himself out of his warm and comfortable bed. After a quick shower and some breakfast, he packed his rucksack for the gym where he was to meet friends, after work, for their weekly training session to prepare for the forthcoming London marathon. Within thirty minutes he was making his way down the High Street towards the underground station, looking every bit the city whiz kid that he had become. He enjoyed the trappings of success, the expensive shirts, the tailor made suits and most of all, the compulsory Blackberry.

"Morning, Charlie," he said, as he paid the street vendor for his daily copy of the Financial Times.

"Any hot tips for today?" enquired Charlie.

"Shell is looking good. They're about to announce record profits, and they're also opening up new sites in Alaska," replied Roberto, giving out information that some would have considered to be insider trading.

He boarded the train, took a seat in the relatively empty compartment and began to read the headlines about London security being tightened, due to the recent bus bombings, when he noticed a discarded magazine on the adjacent seat. He decided that he was too tired to digest any serious news and picked up the woman's journal for some light reading to pass the journey. Like most men, he went straight to the problem page where a married woman was complaining that her husband failed to give her the attention that she felt she deserved. Apparently they had been together for more than twenty years and lived with their two teenage children and she wanted to know whether she should leave him. Roberto wondered how any woman could decide her future based on the detached views of a complete stranger, someone who obviously didn't even know all the facts. However any further thoughts on the subject were quickly dismissed as the train arrived at Canary Wharf.

A ten minute walk took him to the Morgan Stanley building where he worked as an analyst, specialising in oil and gas. Today was going to be a stressful day, as shares had fallen sharply over the entire sector and he was required to make a decision on whether to invest in Venezuelan oil shares. Pressure had been mounting from head office in New York, and he realised, understandably, that in his type of job, people have to make decisions based on the options available to them. If there were no options, no decision needs to be made, but when there's more than one option, as in this case, a choice has to be made. He also knew that any prevarication could cost the firm millions, and consequently affect both his bonus and his job. He had his eye on a second hand Aston Martin and a good bonus would make it a distinct possibility.

He switched on his computer, and as it went through the routine checks and downloads, he noticed that Mary was back at her desk. She had been on special leave after her Mother had been involved in a car crash over two months ago.

"Hello, Mary, how's your Mother now?" he asked, even though he didn't know her that well.

"Mum passed away three weeks ago," she replied. "She never regained consciousness from the car accident. Eventually we decided that she should be allowed a dignified death, so we agreed with the doctors to switch off the life support machines."

"I'm really sorry to hear that," he said. "It must have been a traumatic experience for all of you."

"The hardest part was when the doctor told us that there was no hope. She looked so peaceful, as if she were just asleep; yet the decision to turn off the machine was a lot easier than I thought it would be."

"It's not a decision that I would want to have to make," he said as he hugged her, repeated his condolences and moved back to his desk.

The rest of the day was spent monitoring the worldwide oil and gas share prices and making transatlantic conference calls to his associates in New York. Finally, towards the end of the day, he backed his judgement, and on behalf of his employers spent three million pounds on the Venezuelan oil shares. It was a brave decision as many of his colleagues believed that world requirements for oil would drop during these recessionary times and lead to further price cuts.

"An hour working up a sweat in the gym will help to reduce my stress levels, so see you all in the morning," he said, as he left the office. "Let's hope the demand for oil rockets overnight and we make a few bob on this one."

The gym was only two stops away on the tube but Roberto knew that he needed to hurry if he was going to arrive on time to meet his friends. He rushed down the escalators towards the train, unaware that he was being followed by two policemen. They had noticing him looking extremely anxious while running with a rucksack on his back. One of them called out for him to stop, but in the rush hour noise and confusion, it was impossible for him to hear. His lack of experience, along with the absence of any credible guidance from his superiors, forced the police man into making a decision that couldn't be justified in any civilised society. A few seconds later, just as Roberto reached the door of the carriage, two shots rang out, and he fell into the lap of a middle aged woman. She screamed first, and then cradled his bleeding head in her arms for the remaining moments of his promising life, as he tried to comprehend what had happened to him.

A Mediterranean complexion, an old tattered rucksack and an armed policeman, who valued the victim's life cheaply, were the deciding factors that decreed that an innocent young man, with everything to live for, should be so brutally and callously murdered by the state. To compound the crime, justice was then sidelined, as the morally corrupt head of the security services, along with elements of the gutter press, began a propaganda war to justify the shameful events that led to Roberto's unnecessary death.

The Cost of Oil

Imran wipes away a tear
Tries hard not to show his fear,
They killed my sister
They raped her first
All this for oil, pray quench your thirst.

The bloody soldiers came and went
And left our home broken and bent.
In they stormed
Machine guns cracking
Some children fell, their speed was lacking.

Another notch, the gun's too small
Another killing, just watch him fall.
The oil is ours
You've got your own
You even manage blood from stone.

Dead bodies lying all around
GI's laugh, the only sound.
A baby here
An uncle there
Behind the house, my sister bare.

The New York Times, the caption read
Brave soldiers fought, insurgents dead.
You used your tanks
You fought with skill
You could have talked, but chose to kill.

The world is scared, have some compassion
Your greed grows huge, heed calls to ration.
The land of the free
And home of the brave
Is sending the world to an early grave.

Anna Dobbin

Anna is from Magherafelt. When she was at primary school, Anna took an interest in writing poetry. However after leaving primary school she did not write for many years.

In 2005 Anna began attending creative writing classes which provided her with renewed inspiration and ideas for her writing. These classes led to the formation of the Burnavon Writers Group, of which Anna is a very faithful and enthusiastic member.

Anna believes that her writing has gone from strength, to strength, thanks to the tuition she has received over the past five years.

Uncle Matt's

"Do you want to go to Matt's with me?" my Dad asked. As I was always ready for the road, and to this day still am, I excitedly said, "Yes!" for I loved the great outdoors, and I would certainly find it there, in the heart of the countryside. I got on the bar of the Raleigh bike, which was padded with a couple of big fluffy cushions to make the journey as comfortable as possible. I was in my prime, about seven years old, and off we went; I was as pleased as Punch.

My Dad often told me a story about someone giving him a sixpence (which I gathered was a wee fortune in by-gone days), when he was a child. To keep it safe, as he thought, he discreetly hid it away in a little crevice in the pig-sty at the corner of Uncle Matt's house. Years elapsed and he suddenly remembered about it one day and he went in hot pursuit of the 'tanner' as it was sometimes called. Sadly he never found it. It had gone down memory lane I guess, or meandered its way down a hole in the crumbling wall!

But, back to the earlier part of my story! Matt called me in for tea. What followed was difficult for me to cope with. He stood at the table with one of those big unsliced loaves and went on to cut it into slices, which were as thick as a plank, for Dad and me. The bread was then plastered with country butter, not very appetising to my taste buds. I had to put a plan in motion and my brain worked overtime trying to find a way to dispose of the bread, without being found out. A little voice inside my head was prompting me to crumble the bread and butter into the ashes of the heath fire and shuffle it with the poker and the fire would then, hopefully, make it disappear forever.

This I duly did, and lo and behold my nightmare ended. For the remainder of the evening I felt very uneasy for having committed such a crime for we were always told waste not want not, I thought I was home and dry and was happy as a bee in June as my crime would be forever buried in the ashes. Thou shall not be found out - alas, this was not to be. A volcano erupted. My Uncle discovered what I had done, for he heard a sizzling noise coming from the fire. Of course it was the melting butter which caused this noise. The sermon which followed is still ringing in my ears!

Not to worry - that was many moons ago and I'm still around to tell the tale.

Twine

No matter where I wander around the busy farm
I like a length or two of twine hanging on my arm.
Every farmer knows the tricks-
Whatever is broken, twine will fix.
If there's a hole in the wire, sheep coming through-
Tie it up and it will look like new.
A piece of twine is as precious as gold
Keeping together a gate that's rusty and old.
You might have to make up a pen very quick;
If you didn't have twine you'd feel very sick.
It would secure the corners of the pen for you;
Try it out and you'll see that it's true.
If you've no buttons on your coat and the wife hasn't time to sew,
Wrap some twine around your waist and you'll be ready to go.
So all you farmer friends of mine
Make sure your pockets are stuffed with twine.
It is one of the assets about a farm-
Some lengths of twine hanging over your arm.

www.com etc

www.com is all you ever hear
All to speed things up for us it is made crystal clear.
The web site seems to be the only way.
I'd rather get a handwritten letter than an e-mail any day.
Suppose I'll surf the net some day to keep up with the human race
Though it could disturb forever my very snug little place.
A holiday can be booked with a click on the mouse
Or an e-mail sent from your very own house.
I'm a staunch supporter of the handwritten letter;
To write one and receive one makes me feel much better.
So www. or whatever you like
Regards from me; get on your bike!

Anna Dobbin **23**

Herbie's on a Saturday Night

Etched in my memory from days of yore
Are thoughts of Herbie's grocery store.
I was fascinated by its old-world charm
As I went to do the messages with a basket on my arm.
I would go there every week and was so full of pride
When I spied the goods on display as I quickly stepped inside.
I always thought the owner had crocks and crocks of gold.
He never had any trouble getting his groceries sold.
The money was rolling in very fast to stock up in the bank
So in future years when retired, Herbie'd be able to act the swank.
When I went to get weekly supplies I forgot about the clock.
Then Herbie gave the counter quite a loud knock.
He wanted to draw my attention – I was next in the queue!
As I had other plans in mind , I told him what to do.
"Mr Harkness," I said to him, "there is no need to hurry.
For you must be warned that you 'never hurry a Murray'!"
I was prepared to wait for a while
So the grocer gave me a pleasant smile.
In those days of long ago not a supermarket was in view.
The local grocer supplied the goods and a relaxed friendship grew.
Eventually I got sorted out with sugar, tea and rice
As well as many other items. Then I was told the price.
This brought me to my senses as I stood in the middle of the floor.
So I paid up promptly and headed for the door.
My mother always thought that I was never coming back.
I always told her that I loved to hear the crack.
And as well I liked to swing around the tall pole in the shop
Until my head got very light and then I had to stop.
So my mother was resigned at last that she would have a wait,
For when I went to Herbie's, I'd not be back 'til late.
Even the customers got to know that time for me stood still
As I stared at a little robin perched on the window sill.
Now for me it's off to the supermarket, quickly in and out.
You would probably be arrested if you happened to hang about.
There are cameras located everywhere in case you'd make a raid
And flee far from the superstore before your goods were paid.
Shoppers feel like criminals, and that never can be right.
Oh, I wish I could go shopping to Herbie's on a Saturday night.
Everything then was just spot on.
What a pity that those days are gone.

Childhood Memories

In the peaceful seclusion of the countryside facing Slieve Gallion Braes,
Is my father's birthplace, Glenmaquil, where I spent many happy days,
My memory takes me back in time when I sat on a stool by the fire,
Drinking tea from a blue and white mug, it was my heart's desire.

The pussy cat was purring, with its tail wrapped round its legs,
Matt went out to have a look if the hens had laid their eggs,
Pat would go with a bucket to draw water from the well,
And I closely followed him down the 'little fairy dell'.

This to me was splendour with lilacs swaying in the breeze,
Life was so much simpler then, the folk were all at ease.
Everyone got their day's work done without any fuss or bother,
And always had a lot of time to chat to one another.

As the evening wore on, Matt made the tea
For Pat, for himself, for Dad and for me.
Then I'd go to the door and take a look around
At the beauty of nature everywhere. Then I'd be homeward bound.

Dad's bike was leaned against the wall.
I got up on the bar, I was not very tall.
As we rode off I recalled the events of the day
On a long clear evening in the month of May.

Children now have memories of holidays in sunny Spain,
But I prefer the country life in sunshine or in rain
It gives me lots of pleasure and I reminisce with joy,
On my frequent visits to Glenmaquil, where my father lived as a boy.

The Mobile Phone.

The mobile phone is the plague of my life,
It cuts at my being like a carving knife.
No matter where I go the mobile goes as well,
Ringing often in my ears with its very demanding bell.
His "nibs" said I needed one because I'm travelling so much.
"You are better to have one with you so you can keep in touch."
I suppose my car could break down on the busy M6.
Without my phone, I must admit, I'd really be in a fix.
The other day I went to Tina's tea room for a tasty snack,
And to sit and have a little rest and ease the pain in my back,
I sat down in the friendly surroundings to enjoy my cup of tea,
Delighted because I thought I had the afternoon free.
No such luck - the mobile rang and I jumped to attention,
I had to go and do some jobs, sure I'd be better off on the pension.
Even the teenagers and children have phones pressed to their ears,
Despite the constant warning about possible health fears.
Parents often buy them, to keep up with the Jones,
To pacify their moaning kids, they get them mobile phones.
There's Motorola, Orange and Nokia too.
From the vast selection, I name only a few,
New ones appear from time to time with free call minutes galore,
The one I have will do me, I don't want any more.
What did folk do years ago, no such gadget was in sight?
As far as I can gather, they did perfectly alright,
If I could be granted one wish it would be,
To throw my mobile phone far away from me.
Give me space for just one day,
Mobile madness go away,
So I can go for a walk on the fells
Without the persistent ringing of telephone bells.
Since I mastered texting a few years ago,
My spelling has gone to the dogs ye know.
These are my thoughts on the mobile phone,
For a while I want peace and to be left alone.

Carol Doey

Carol loves entertaining people; she is passionate about storytelling, drama, the theatre and most of all, about writing. She is an accomplished playwright, who has written and staged several very successful productions. Through the Open Door Theatre Group, which Carol set up three years ago, she has heightened local interest in drama on both participant and audience levels.

Carol loves to nudge other people into fulfilling their dreams.

She says, "I love the journey we take collectively to arrive at our destination; no amount of money can buy that feeling of satisfaction."

Gone in a Puff

As Phyllis Nelson drew the evening to an end with *Move Closer* bodies clung to each other like limpets. The heady scents of aftershave, perfume and testosterone filled the ballroom. A haze of bluish smoke hovered beneath the mirrored ball. My head rested awkwardly on my partner's clavicle. I dared not move for fear of breaking the spell. Indeed many a spell was cast and many a prayer prayed to snare this fine specimen I was resting on. As I inhaled his fading Faberge, Phyllis exhaled her last note. He held me at arm's length, then slowly pulled me to him. On that nine-second journey my heart raced, legs buckled and pelvic muscles tightened ...... our lips met .... well, his met mine first. He cast his top lip out, catching mine, as a camel would suck leaves off a bush. We guzzled for what seemed like a lifetime.

When I opened my eyes the barman had called time and, with the exception of the odd inebriated soul groping their way to the exit, we were the only patrons left. The draught from every exit congregated round my calves, leaving me frozen from the waist down. From the waist up I was at boiling point. I was happy when my conquest led me to his car where, on the way to his house, my legs thawed.

A fine house it was – much too big for a bachelor. He opened the door and switched on the light.

"Tea or coffee?" he asked.

"Coffee, please," I replied. "Where is your bathroom?"

He nodded to a door at the top of the stairs. Feeling full of fluid I climbed the stairs sharply. Relieving myself I scanned the surroundings. I spied mouthwash. A swig of that will freshen my breath, I thought. Rising from the bowl I noticed a tin of talc. Before zipping I lifted the tin to dust a little on my skin. Before I knew it I was amid plumes of white smoke; the lid had come off and the contents were lying in the gusset of my Sloggis, those comfortable heavy-duty knickers.

This could not be happening! To reach this night had taken months of careful planning, crash diets and Machiavellian plotting. To see it all go up in a puff of Old English Lavender would be soul destroying. I waddled to the toilet to empty the gusset but the Lycra acted as a catapult. Clouds of heavily scented talc filled the air. Flapping the talc out of the window, I did not hear the door opening; but I heard a cough. I spun round and there he stood. Stepping forward to explain I lost him in a cloud of smoke that wafted from my trouser leg. When the dust settled, we faced each other.

He had a light film of talc on his fringe and eyebrows.

It didn't take a Cherokee Indian to read the real smoke signals that said:
Close the door on your way out!

Growing Up

Rose Bradley always felt far removed from her family. As she stood half in
and half out of the makeshift pigsty, her subconscious was recording the
events, events that would be replayed many times throughout her life.

From an early age Rose had this feeling that she was different from her
siblings. She grew up in a three bedroom terraced house. Rose was the
third of six. The first, a boy, had been stillborn. The second was a girl, the
apple of her father's eye. Rose was next and, in her mother's words, "reared
herself". Two more girls followed, then the son.

Her parents were very strict. They demanded nothing more than, or less
than the Waltons. Looking back it seemed they had a vision of the perfect
family....... the nurse, the hairdresser, the policewoman, the teacher. The
son would follow his father's footsteps. He was a hard working mechanic
who loved the lambeg drum. The daughters would each marry a Protestant
farmer and the son would marry a hard working, child bearing Protestant
girl. Their vision was spot on, on four accounts.

The night the sow died was traumatic for Rose. It was the night the
conclusive seed was firmly sown, that she was different. It seemed that
nobody else cared about the sow's demise. The actual death was bad
enough, but what made it worse was knowing the sow was gone forever,
leaving the piglets with no mother. It was the cruel and callous way she was
scoffed at for crying sore about a sow. Rose watched her father and the vet
haul the sow from the crate and dump her unceremoniously in the corner of
the sty.

The seed was well and truly fertilised and boy did it grow!

The sow was but a memory the night her grandfather, her father's father,
died. The time and place were all wrong. Her grandfather had lived with
them for the last couple of years and, much to the annoyance of his
daughter in law and of Rose's siblings, she and her grandfather had
become firm friends. Each night Rose would read from his big, green bible
and when she had finished she would tell him her secrets and he would

smile. On this particular night he found it hard to catch his breath.

Rose went for her father. The doctor was called and he decided to send for an ambulance. Rose cried inconsolably as they carried him out. Her mother allayed her fears by telling her he was going to a good place to get better.

The days that followed were harrowing for the child and undoubtedly played a part in moulding this eleven year old into the rebel that she would become. On the day Rose did her Leaving Certificate her favourite person in the whole world died. Her father came to school to break the news; he must have loved her when he came himself and for this she would be eternally grateful. She knew he was grief stricken. He encircled the steering wheel with his two big arms and hung his head.

Rose cried for her grandfather; she cried for her father; and how she envied that steering wheel. She was devastated and the world and everyone in it would pay dearly. She was filled with hate and anger. She would never trust anyone again. Authority she loathed, and did everything in her power to be loathed back. If it were the in thing to be white, then Rose Bradley would be sprayed black! She couldn't express her feelings; she was only a child. She had no say in this house, a house where you were hugged with a wet dish cloth or a sally rod. Feelings of emptiness and loneliness would sweep over her in waves. How she missed the man she loved and who had loved her unconditionally.

The wake and funeral were the beginning of her claustrophobia, which she suffers from to this day. On and on came a string of people – shaking hands, drinking tea. Rose was allowed to stay. Her siblings were farmed out to relatives and neighbours. She watched people to and fro for two nights. They stroked her head as though she were a cat. If only she had been a cat, she could have disappeared. Although she was heart sore she was glad to have been allowed to stay. Rose followed her father around the house, always staying a discreet distance away, watching his every move. The child was crying out for his love. She wanted them to grieve together. The funeral service in the house is as vivid today as it was then.

She had parked herself on the stairs where she could see her father. A vicar hovered. The front door was opened wide. A bitter draught was heading straight to her legs. Men in dark suits stood in the hall and spilled out onto the street. They spoke in low, serious tones. Rose poked at little bits of wood from the wallpaper, her eyes never leaving her father's face. Her fingers were raw, as slivers of wood chip pierced the nail beds. She felt no pain.

The Lord is my shepherd; I shall not want.

Yea, though I walk through the valley of death, I will fear no evil.

During the wake she had perfected her peripheral vision so she was able to see her mother cross the kitchen with an empty mug and her aunt write a card at the table whilst never missing a body movement of her father. He stood in the doorway of the room where her grandfather's body lay. Someone coughed loudly. It must have been a signal because a hush fell on the whole street. All eyes, with the exception of Rose's, turned to the vicar. Hers were on her father. It was somewhere between *the valley of death* and *a staff and rod comforting ye* that she saw her father put his big, calloused hand, all rough from his work as a mechanic, into the top pocket of his jacket and pull out a brilliant white handkerchief. Rose held her breath. It was as if someone had slowed down the world. She watched as the handkerchief went up to his eyes. He dabbed each one briefly and ran the cloth above his cheekbones, then wiped his nose before putting the handkerchief back in his pocket.

The ache in her heart was indescribable. The searing pain she felt as she watched her father cry made her retch. She felt so lonely.
Rose Bradley stepped onto the stairway of life the night the sow died. The night her grandfather died she realised it was moving.

Revenge – Hell Hath No Fury!

At the third attempt I managed to unscrew the lid of my flask. The jerking action caused a spot or two of warm milk to land on the back of my hand. I mopped it with my tongue, never being one to waste anything that would line my stomach. I was neither hungry nor thirsty; the warm coffee was a means to defrost me from the inside out. I was on a lay by on the route of a cycle race. I was at checkpoint number three with a boot load of bananas, Mars bars and water to be handed, flung or fired at the cyclists on their way past. I could not believe this was seven a.m. on a Sunday morning. I should have been turning over in my king size bed for a second sleep.

I was at an auction many years ago and I ended up with a fireside chair, three suitcases and a coal scuttle, all because I acknowledged a neighbour in the crowd. I carried a large wooden cross one Good Friday all around our village because the man who always carried it got shingles when his wife left him; he was stressed and asked for my help. I just couldn't refuse. So be it with this check point. Etched on my mind from previous relationships were the words 'refusal often offends'. So as we lay entwined on my king size bed, I got sentimental and offered my services. Or got mental and offered my services. This has been my life to date; I do things I don't want to because I can't say no. I don't do things that I want to because I can't say yes. I have full scale conversations with people I don't know, just to make them feel wanted. There's no point going into the finer details of my inability to conduct life in a semi-normal manner except to say was my own my own fault that I was standing there alone and frozen to the core.

As I poured the milk on top of the Arabic coffee my nostrils expanded as the overpowering aroma hovered in the cool air. I gathered the mug in both hands and the thaw was instant. I eyed the boot, or rather eyed the Mars bars in the boot, and yet another bane of my life began to torment me. Coffee without Mars, coffee with Mars, half a Mars with coffee – the saliva gathered and the chocolate was melting as I pondered. I heard the quiet whoosh of a gentle breeze. I've never heard angel wings but I'm sure that's what they would have sounded like. I spun around to see if Gabriel or Raphael had left their calling feather. No feather, but a multitude of cyclists in formation, like wild geese migrating. Synchronised pedalling and I had missed it drooling over chocolate.

I knew Harold wouldn't be in that group as he wasn't a fully fledged cyclist yet. He had all the gear: tight lycra shorts with matching jersey, helmet, goggles, water bottle..... He just needed a bit more practice. He was ever so upset when his wife bought the bike one Christmas and insisted he go out on it at least three times a week, telling him he was a couch potato. Harold was livid and one day, over shepherd's pie and spring cabbage, confided to me his wife's bullying tactics. My heart went out to him. He was a lovely, kind, caring man who worked hard and provided well for his family and didn't need the someone who was supposed to love him *till death us do part* scoffing at his lack of toned muscle. Anyway he said he felt released after his chat with me and asked if I would like to see his allotment some evening.

Harold was very much into organic vegetables. He was proud of them so I couldn't understand why, when he was eating healthily, and enabling his family to do so too, that his wife couldn't praise him instead of persecuting him. The allotment was the start of an organic relationship. As he guided me up and down the furrows with his rough calloused hands on my elbow I never felt anything like the electricity that surged through my being. As we made a right turn at the bottom of the broad bean patch somehow we ended up facing each other. I was glad I had on my rubber boots. These kept me firmly grounded and safe from the electrocution that may have occurred otherwise. And the rest, as they say, is history.

I closed the boot to avoid temptation or missing the next multitude of cyclists or, more importantly, Harold. I hadn't seen much of him lately as he was out training almost every night for this big charity cycle and, as he said, he couldn't divide himself. Margaret from work had bought a bicycle and he had shown her the ropes a few times – how to change gears, for example. Seemingly you had to be quick changing gears as you approached a hill or you'd have to walk up it. First of all I was sort of jealous. I mean I know he had a wife, but that was different – they were no longer talking, had separate rooms and, as Harold said on more than one occasion, it would soon be separate houses. But Margaret was a single mother and tended to be a bit of a latch, all eyelash blinking and coy smiles. Harold said he didn't want to be in a room alone with her as he felt she was a girl who didn't have a good reputation. So that settled the feeling of discomfort I'd had when I saw her leaning against him in the queue at the canteen.

My boot was getting lighter with each cyclist that passed. I'd stand near the edge of the road with water in one hand and a banana and a Mars bar in the other. When the cyclist was within earshot I'd roar, "Would you like a drink or a bar?" Most amateurs would stop for a break and have some provisions, while the professionals would waft past, heads down, bottoms up.

Now patience is a virtue, but mine was wearing thin and I was getting restless. Every now and then a lone cyclist would trundle past but Harold was nowhere to be seen. Maybe he had been knocked off his bicycle and was lying heels up in a ditch; or had taken a heart attack and had been rushed off by air ambulance to the nearest hospital. As these negative thoughts swam around my head a vision appeared out of the morning haze. A ray of sun had forced its way through the clouds to light the path for my Harold. I recognised the burnt orange jersey and matching helmet.

I was ecstatic. The corners of my mouth were stretched to capacity. The burnt orange was a magnet for my eyes. Squinting from the sun, I caught a mere glimpse of fuchsia pink on Harold's left side. As he drew near the pink phantom evolved from a spiritual aura to Margaret from work. Harold had never mentioned that she'd be there. From jubilation to desolation in a split second! I was fixed to the tarmac, my world crumbling around me. There I stood like Doc Holliday, a banana in each hand. Both cycles passed in a whoosh. Harold kept his head down while Margaret's eyes vacuumed the last crumb of my self-worth. As they faded from my view, I turned to close the boot. Before putting the bananas back in their box I slowly brought them to my lips. I puffed a short burst of air into each banana. Doc Holliday would have been so proud!

Driving towards the village I couldn't believe the calmness that surrounded me. I parked my car outside the bakery, waving at the girls. I headed towards the centre. I turned left before the butcher's and started the journey uphill to the allotment. I was slightly out of breath passing Mrs Harkness's braying donkeys.

It only took fifteen minutes, well, twenty five altogether, to tidy up the loose ends. I started my descent towards the village. I had a spring in my step as I thought of the fete on Saturday. Harold always came first in the organic section. His perfectly formed aubergines and celeriac won the hearts of the judges every year.

This year will be slightly different though. From one half of his aubergines and celeriac I carved a basket of perfectly shaped reminders of our sultry nights in the allotment shed. I sprayed them a striking fuchsia pink. The other half kept Mrs Harkness's donkeys from braying for a while.

As you cycle through life, Harold, remember, "You reap what you sow." and may the only hearts you break in future be those of your celeriac!

Huggin'

I hate it, I hate it, I hate it... people who do it should be arrested and put in a room with earwigs and old men who clougher....*and* it's the *in* thing now… everybody who is somebody does it…they come at you like some deranged creature, arms outstretched, teeth and gums on display to the recipient and anyone in the vicinity....It's called hugging....AND I HATE IT! You're supposed to do it at least once a day…seemingly its great for your wellbeing…If you haven't seen someone in a while; they feel it necessary to molest you with one of these horrendous suffocating acts. Doing someone a favour now constitutes a vice like grip, and salivating on your clavicle at the same time. Or may God help you if you have a personal problem and the huggers find out…they'll lean on you until they leave an imprint of themselves on your body…like a big postmark…
Hugging didn't exist when I was growing up…a wallop with a wet dish cloth or a sally rod on the back of the legs was the nearest thing to a hug in our house…So don't invade my space with your newfangled greeting method… A simple "Hello" "Thank you" or an "I'm here for you" will suffice…I prefer people with big bellies or long noses because they don't get so close to you…and next time someone comes at me with the intention of invading my privacy with the dreaded hug, clinch, embrace or whatever swanky title you give it…be warned… I will have a wet kipper in my pocket and I shall leave you with an imprint…and it won't be from a hug!

Joyce Doris

Joyce grew up in a rural town in Northern Ireland. She is trained as a teacher and is married to Eugene - they have six children.

Joyce recalls that during her childhood discipline was the order of the day in school and at home. People took great care not to offend their neighbours and children knew their place.

Through her writing Joyce hopes to show how the human spirit can remain undaunted in the face of challenge. She uses humour in her work believing that laughter heals many wounds.

Just Like Me

There she was, someone just like me - my one and only daughter, crying at the kitchen table; being comforted by her new fiance Chris.

"Mary! What's wrong?" I barely heard my own voice.
"Oh, I've a sore stomach," she struggled to reply.

Suddenly that horrible clammy cramp-like feeling returned from the past and coursed through my veins. I knew instantly what the matter was - we had been arguing over the wedding guest list. My mind wandered back over the years and I recalled the aggravation concerning who was to be invited. I had over one hundred on my list and still there were people offended at not getting an invitation.

"You can't leave out my first cousins," I had pleaded, " Mammy and Daddy, God rest him, were at all their weddings with some of us. Your father and I were at Tom Quinn's wedding with your Aunty Margaret."

"But I don't know any of them; and if I invite them I will have too many people for Parkanaur," she remonstrated.

"Parkanaur?" I thought, "Why can't she book the Greenvale or the Glenavon beside her like the rest of the people. Numbers wouldn't be a problem and you could be cut in two going out on that Ballygawley Road."

I backed out of the room and later I slid guiltily back into the kitchen to find Chris on his own.

He spoke and dropped a hint as light as a snowflake but coated in honey.
"You know you like to be in charge don't you?"
I had to answer, "Yes, I do." I was never more aware of my slow, sad voice. "Why do people make you answer?" I winced.

The next day as they were leaving for London, I said airily at breakfast:
"You know, Mary, I was thinking; leave out the Quinns and my first cousins and take Parkanaur. It's beautiful. I'll ring Marlene today if you like. People won't mind; sure some of Polly's children went abroad to get married."
Surprised, she began to object, but my mind was made up. I was surprised how content I felt.

A week later she texted to say:
Have booked Belfast Castle - numbers no problem Mary x

An Interview

Rural bar (80s)

Two young men and a girl, Michael, John and Mary, enter a bar.

Michael: Hello. How're you doing? I'll take two pints of harp and a glass of orange juice, please.

Barman: Right ye are! *(pours drink)* It's a wild nice day that, eh?

Michael: Aye right enough. Listen thanks. *(returns to the table)*

John: Do you see them boys over there in the corner – they're watching us

Michael: They're looking at the car - not a bit slow. *(laughs)*

Mary: There's nobody here. Did you see that sign? There is no band tonight. I'm away to the bathroom.

(Michael goes up to the bar. The barman has returned from the yard with a crate of minerals)

Michael: I'll take the same again.

Barman: Right! Is that your Fiat Uno out there, do ye mind me asking?

Michael: No not at all. The red one? It's my mother's I haven't got one of my own.

Barman: They're a great wee car them. My sister has one this years and it never let her down yet. I see you bought it off Paddy Young. Are ye a Moneymore man yourself?

Michael: I am, aye. I know Paddy well. I went to school with his son Dickie.

Local on barstool: They say Moneymore going there and moneyless coming back ha!

Michael: *(joining in the joke and laughing)* Aye especially if you're buying a car.

Barman: Tell me this, how's that pub the Beer Kellar doing? Your man is doing a quare trade they tell me.

Michael: 'Oh John's left that pub now; he's just out at the house now.

Barman: You're coddin! That's a good un, hi.'

(Michael returns to the table)

Michael: I was just having a bit of crack with the barman. He was talking about Moneymore.

Mary: Did you not tell him who you were? He probably knows Daddy.

Michael: I did not indeed; I'm not telling my business. Anyway we're goin' after this drink.

Mary: Ach, you know countrymen; they just like to know who they're talking to.

John: *(glancing about)* They don't like Moneymore boys here, ye know. They're giving us some looks in that corner; we could get a hiding yet. *(laughs)*

(Silence, then John breaks into a tune)

John: There may be troubles ahead, there may be …moonlight and music and love and romance. Let's face the music and dance.

(Laughter from corner).

I Don't Think I Could Live With You Again

I don't think I could live with you again.
We never met, but while he slept; I pained
For fear you might escape from your dark den;
Kept watch in bed, eyes burning as ears strained.
I felt the danger to my sleeping son.
It takes a thief to catch a thief, they say.
I became like you as time ticked on
Ruthless, I set poison and traps by day.

One night the deadly poison took its grip.
Sick and scraping sounds became subdued.
He's dead now, he joked but I, tightlipped,
Thought how you might feel for a helpless brood.
Torn, fighting tooth and nail; the female
Of the species is more deadly than the male.

February

'February brings the rain'. Even the words of the popular nursery rhyme do not bring the usual cheeriness.

February is the second month in the Georgian calendar and gets its name from a period of purification rather like lent - Februa was the ancient Roman feast of purification.

My birthday is on the sixteenth of February; my age is now classified information! Lately I read an old Irish saying:
'An bhean a inis leat cen aois se, inseoidh se rud ar bith'
A woman who tells you her age will tell you anything.

Birthdays are a time when I take stock. An old school friend, Dympna Burns, passed away recently. I never saw her since primary school days but I heard she went to England, married over there and became a school principal. Dympna would have been a conscientious principal, but to me she will always be the gentle ladylike girl with the waist length hair who sat behind me in Master Brady's classroom. 'We are all the richer for knowing Dympna' I wrote in the Mass card to her mother. With a lump in my throat the words were chosen as carefully as precious stones.

For the first time now, I am older than my sister was before she passed away from cancer. I have no chiding star to guide me. A friend has recently appointed herself to be my new life coach. She has taken to advising me with the tact and predictability of a modern Lady Bracknell. When I hear the words:

'Now, Joy, I know you are a great girl BUT'......' I find myself open mouthed, clenching the receiver like a vice, bracing myself for what's coming next.

February! I'll brace it rather than embrace it.

Malcolm Duffey

A native of the Sandholes district, Malcolm is a retired Secondary School Principal.

During a long teaching career he took a particular interest in History, Literature and Drama, often writing scripts and producing school musicals and pantomimes. His interest in Drama also extended to involvement within local church groups.

Malcolm has also been a part-time photographic journalist, covering local events for several weekly newspapers.

Retirement has given him the opportunity to develop his writing skills through acting as Chairman of a Development Association, an Historical Society and as Secretary to several organisations.

It has also uncovered a latent talent for short story writing, particularly about the humour and idiosyncrasies of country life.

Let Down

Bob bounced the ball as he watched the man paste the poster on the weather beaten fence. It covered several other faded and torn ones advertising past events. Bob kicked the ball to his friend Joe who, for once, ignored it, as he tried to read the words as they were unrolled and fastened by several quick strokes of the brush.

"The Mighty" he began slowly.
"The Mighty Marvo - Zulu Chief," prompted Bob. "in the Town Hall."
"When?" asked Joe.
"Hold on - wait till the man gets the poster up."
"That'll be smashin'. When's he coming?"
"On Friday 22nd October at 8.00pm," Bob read.
"How much to get in?"
"Admission 2/6 - children HALF PRICE."
"How much is that Bob?" Joe enquired impatiently.
"It's one and three pence."
"Och, where would I get that?"
"You may ask your Da."
"There'd be no chance - you know what he would say! Hey Mister, any free tickets?"

The man lifted his bucket and stood back to admire his handiwork as if the boys didn't exist.
"Hey Mister!"
He turned towards the van. "I hope you boys won't tear that down."
"Now why would we want to do that?" enquired Bob innocently.
"We'll look after it - see that no-one touches it." offered Joe.

"I tell you what I'll do - I'll give you two free tickets if you can look after this poster and get all your friends to come."
"No bother, Mister - we'll even put up a few more posters if you want."
The man opened the back door of his van, and took out a roll of posters and a packet of paste. He handed them to Joe.

"Well that seems a fair exchange - make sure they are displayed where they can be seen."
"As good as done!" said Joe.

The man closed the rear door of the van and made towards the driver's seat. Joe followed - "What about the tickets?" he enquired.
"I have them right here." - he reached into the glove compartment and unearthed the tickets.

"Thanks very much Mister - Come on, Bob, we've got work to do." He tucked the posters under one arm and made off towards the town centre. Bob gathered up the football and ran to catch up.

The next few days were spent poster pasting and ensuring that everybody knew about the visit of the Great Marvo. They could guarantee the Town Hall would be packed, but the matter of the free tickets was a closely guarded secret.

Bob and Joe's passion for football took a back seat as they both eagerly awaited the appearance of the Great Marvo. Their teacher, Miss Bennett, was more than suspicious when both were found in the library at break time rather than their normal football which they played no matter the weather. She found it hard to come to terms with their fascination, indeed obsession, for African customs and culture.

At last the day of the concert dawned and amongst the early arrivals, presenting their tickets at the box office were the two pals. Neither of them had ever been to a show before and even a visit to the Town Hall seemed unreal. They were awestruck by the size of the amphitheatre with its dimmed lights, the heavy velvet curtains, the carpet, the plush seats. It was difficult to decide where to sit and after several changes they finally settled near the central aisle with a good view of the stage. Here they soaked in the atmosphere with its excited chatter and background music as the hall filled.

Then suddenly, a crescendo of drums, the lights dimmed, the curtains opened, the spotlights lit up the stage and there was a majestic troupe of native dancers, pulsating, gyrating to the beat of the drums. The noise and tempo increased, the dancers stamped wildly, and there was the Great Marvo magnificent in his bearing, master of the stage.

Over the next two hours the audience was held spellbound as the story unfolded of courage and triumph over disasters both natural and human, but above all the pulsating energy and kaleidoscopic colour. Then with a final ear splitting-roll of the drums the curtain closed, the house lights came on and the audience blinked. Bob and Joe walked home in silence, the noise still ringing in their ears, fireworks going off in their heads.

"See you in the morning," said Joe.
"Yeah," replied Bob as they parted.

They met up later than usual in the open space at the end of the avenue. The posters still hung brightly on the wooden hoarding.
"That was some show - I could go tonight again." said Joe.
"I dunno, I didn't sleep all night. Anyway, it's moving on to somewhere else."

"That must be a great life -I'd love to be a showman and travel the world."
"I thought you wanted to be a footballer?"
"I'm not so sure now - bein' a showman would be more exciting."
"And what would you be? Not another Great Marvo - last year you were going to be another Stanley Matthews!"
"I wonder could we see them before they leave?"
"Are you thinking of going with them?"
"I might."
"Well away you go. I have to go to the butchers for me mam."
"Well afterwards will you come with me?"
"Me mam wants some chops for the dinner and if I don't get back I'll be in trouble."

The two boys set off towards the town's main shopping street where McKee Family Butcher's Shop stood. It was always busy on a Saturday morning as the regulars queued up for their Sunday joints. Terence McKee, cheeks as red as the liver on the slab, and a broad grin, happily kept the queue moving.

"Well Mrs. Arthurs it's the usual I suppose - or are your lodgers staying over the weekend?"
"No. Mr. Samuel is leaving this morning - catching the bus back to Belfast."
"It was a great show last night."
"Yes - you wouldn't think it was the same person. He's a great showman."
"Does he not travel with the rest?"
"No he likes to be by himself. He's a gentleman. Speaks perfect English. I'll have a pound of sausages thank you."

When the two boys emerged from the butcher's shop, Joe gave Bob a sharp dig with his elbow.
"Would you look!" he croaked in amazement. There standing at the bus stop on the opposite side of the street was a tall coloured gentleman, dressed in a long black coat and bowler hat complete with gloves and umbrella, a smart black leather suitcase at his feet.

"So that's the Great Marvo," Joe remarked in disbelief as they made their way back to the estate, trying to come to terms with the discovery.
"Maybe being a footballer's not so bad an idea after all," Bob mused. They had reached the fence where the posters for the Great Marvo hung, fresh and intact.
Joe caught the corner of the poster and pulled. It came away in a long sliver.

"See you later for a kickabout."

The Silver Locket

"This way sir."
The waitress led the way through the crowded dining room, stopping under the central chandelier.
"Your table, sir." She pointed to the Reserved notice. She pulled out a chair. Robert's heart sank as he waited for Kathleen to take her seat. He had asked for a corner table out of the public glare but here they were in a pool of light right in the centre of the room with all eyes on them.
"Nice place this," Kathleen remarked as she took in her surroundings.
"I see Hugh the bread delivery man is here." She smiled across the room, acknowledging his greeting.
"Oh no!" Robert groaned inwardly. He had plucked up courage to ask Kathleen out and he had chosen this restaurant, not expecting to meet any one he knew or be recognised.
"He's sitting over by the wall, " Kathleen directed. Robert let his gaze wander in that direction and was greeted by a broad smile and a knowing wink. He dropped his gaze and felt the heat rise in his cheeks.
"That's the cat out of the bag," he thought to himself. "The news will be all around the country tomorrow morning!"
"I suppose that's his wife?" Kathleen enquired.
"I don't know. I never met her."
"I wouldn't be too sure. He's got a fly eye in his head, has Hugh."
"And what will he say I've got Kathleen?"
"Now don't you worry what other people say. They'll have something to talk about. You invited me out and I accepted. We're out to enjoy ourselves." She reached across the table and placed her hand reassuringly on top of his. "Forget about them" she smiled.

He had got to know Kathleen over several months when she had started calling in his country grocery store. She had come to the district as a decorator, first of all for the Hamiltons and then had moved on to their neighbours and when one was finished she was quickly taken on by another. There was no scarcity of customers ready to engage her services and her friendly personality and easy going attitude certainly helped this along. A young lady painter and decorator was somewhat of a novelty but it also gave plenty of opportunity for the tongue waggers and gossips who were quick to point out the number of elderly bachelors on her clientele list. It set the tongues wagging and the stories flying.

"There's no fool like an old fool" and "A fool and his money are easily parted" were popular phrases when her name came up in conversation. It didn't seem to bother Kathleen as she went about her decorating assignments.

"Would you care to order now?" Robert was woken out of his reverie by the waitress who collected the menu cards and stood with pencil poised above her order list.

"I'll take the melon – I suppose you'd rather have soup?" Kathleen offered.

"Fine by me," Robert replied "and I'll have the steak."

"The Chicken Maryland for me, thanks, and a glass of white wine!"

"How do you like your steak sir?"

"Well done."

"And any drinks?"

"I'll just stick to the water. It's very warm". Robert could feel the heat under his collar. He felt like a moth caught in the beam of a car light as he sat in the full glare of the centre light with all the diners watching them from the semi-darkness. If he could have escaped at that moment he would

He looked across at Kathleen. He had never seen her looking so radiant and vivacious. She was dressed in a smart red dress which complemented her figure. "You're looking nice tonight," he remarked.

"Thanks. Do you like my dress?"

"Lovely – it suits you so well."

She smiled. "I bought it for tonight." He was pleased that she had gone to the trouble of buying a new dress, pleased that she was even bothered to go out with him.

On Kathleen's visits to the shop he had gradually got to know her. She had the habit of lingering until all the customers had left or arriving when there was no one around. At first Robert was uncomfortable and uneasy but her easy patter and friendliness gradually overcame these worries and he looked forward eagerly to her appearance.

Robert had worked in the country stores all his life. First, when his mother was alive he had learnt the grocery trade under her strict regime and then after her death he had simply carried on, falling into a familiar rut and becoming a confirmed bachelor along the way.

The waitress arrived with the soup which was piping hot. Beads of sweat broke out on his forehead.

"It's hot," Kathleen sympathised.

"Aye these lights and now hot soup. I made a wrong choice."

Robert reached into his pocket for his handkerchief. His hand closed on the red velvet box and he looked across at Kathleen. He could picture the silver locket on her delicate neck. He had planned to give the locket to her in a quiet moment when the time and place was right. But this wasn't the right place in the full glare of attention. The silver locket had lain on his mother's dressing table for years. It had been in the family for several generations. "Some day you'll give this necklace to some lucky girl Robert" she pronounced, but never encouraged him in any romantic notion he had. As she grew older she actively discouraged any thoughts he had of marriage, wanting him to devote all his attentions to her welfare. He had come to accept his lot as a lonely bachelor when Kathleen came into his life, but the great gulf in their ages and background made the situation preposterous.

"Your steak, sir."
"And the Chicken Maryland."
The waitress placed the plates on the table, then enquired if anything more was required. Kathleen kept up a patter of conversation which Robert welcomed as he came to terms with the situation.

Hugh the bread man was a regular at his shop, calling twice a week. He was the first with all the news of the district, good or bad, and a story lost nothing in the telling when Hugh got hold of it. When they had finished their meal, Hugh and his wife made a point of coming past Robert's table. "Well you're a dark horse Bob. Didn't expect to see you here. You kept this quiet eh Kathleen?"
"Oh we are here often. Everybody knows that - or they will now!"
"They'll not hear a word from me, isn't that right Mary?"
"Hughie wouldn't tell a soul. Never tells me anything that happens round the country."
"Nice to see people out enjoying themselves, Bob. Have a good evening." They moved off towards the door.
"It'll be all round the country in the morning. He'll tell every house he comes to," Robert admitted.
"Don't worry Robert. It's our own business what we do."
"I can hear them laughing at us."
"I'm not laughing. I came because I wanted to. Now let's forget them all and enjoy the rest of the evening," Kathleen advised.

They finished their meal. The strains of the dance orchestra drifted in from the ballroom. Kathleen grabbed Robert's hand and led him towards the dance floor. He managed to stumble his way awkwardly through a slow foxtrot and gradually the tension drained from his body. Kathleen's presence had such a calming and soothing effect on him.

Later he dropped Kathleen off and drove home. The house was dark and silent, as if disapproving of his being out late. He checked the locks, then took the velvet box out of his pocket. He snapped open the lid and held the delicate chain up to the light then let it run through his fingers, the light glinting on it as it turned. For a few seconds he held the locket between finger and thumb above the dying embers in the grate, then carefully replaced it in its box.

"Maybe another day," he mused out loud, "but tomorrow the craic will start."
He could imagine the talk behind his back.

"If his mother was livin' she'd soon send that one runnin'."

"Sure he's old enough to be her father."

"The wee shop will get the quare scatterin' if she gets her hands on it."

"It's what he deserves, miserable oul' skin flint."

With a sigh Robert climbed the stairs, but there was a contented smile on
his face. There would be another day and maybe, just maybe, they could
plan things better.

Dirty Business

Jack Brown uncoupled the section of suction hose and secured it at the side
of the tanker. He removed his mask and gloves, placed them in their
compartment and climbed into the cab. A glance at his clip board indicated
he had three more calls before knocking off. "Better not tempt providence,"
he mused to himself as he eased the tanker out of the narrow entrance and
into the flow of city bound traffic.

He was looking forward to a spot of fishing. The weather looked promising,
a bit overcast but warm and he had found a quiet pool where there was one
great trout. He nearly had him last time but the darkness and the crafty trout
beat him. This evening just maybe! He licked his lips in anticipation.

"Oh no!" he groaned as his mobile rang. He knew it meant an extra call and
that meant he'd be late and he'd miss that trout again. He swore under his
breath and eased the tanker into a lay-by. Before he could stop the mobile
rang again.

"Jack how are you fixed ? There's an urgent call to the Malone Road."

"I've enough to keep me the rest of the day. It'll have to wait till the
morning."

"Now Jack you can stretch a point – there's some charity do on and the
owner has phoned looking an urgent call out."

"Well they'll have to take their turn in the queue."

"Jack, Mr Harrison has asked that we make a special case for Mrs Basildon-
Blakely."

"Just because she's double barrelled and comes from the Malone Road
doesn't mean she should get priority treatment."

"Just this time, Jack – I'll not forget it."

"You will till there's another of Mr Harrison's pals wanting a favour. It's
against the rules."

"Thanks Jack, I knew I could count on you."

Jack's mood didn't improve as he got caught up in the afternoon school traffic. He swung the tanker into the gravelled drive between the rhododendrons and azaleas, now in full bloom. The drive meandered through an expansive lawn, on which a large marquee had been erected, to the front of an impressive Georgian Mansion.

"Worth a bob or two is Mrs Double Barrel," he thought to himself.

He was climbing down from the cab when he heard the scrunch of feet moving on the gravel. Jack swung round to be confronted by a breathless maid in black dress and white apron.

"Mrs Basildon-Blakely would like you to take your vehicle round the back," she gasped, "She doesn't want the neighbours to see it."

Jack took a deep breath "You can tell Mrs What's her name that if she's worried about what the neighbours see then I can take my tanker off her drive right now. That will suit me very well."

"Oh no! Please don't go. She wants the drains unblocked!"

"Well she should have thought of that sooner."

"She says you're not to park near the pavilion. There's a big fund-raising barbeque this evening and she doesn't want the smell to spoil the event."

Jack looked across the lawn to where a group of caterers were busy laying out tables for the barbeque.

Suddenly there was a shriek "Madame Pompidou! Beau Brummel! Come here – retrieve them, Marianne." The maid instantly gave chase after two poodles, one jet black, the other snow white, which were frisking across the lawn and out of reach, to the shrill shrieks of their agitated owner.

Mrs Basildon-Blakely, dressed in a long blue evening dress and white stole, her chest heaving with the exertion, turned to Jack.

"My good man, I've organised this very important charity event. It will be attended by some very influential people who will be arriving within hours. Mr Henderson assured me the drains would be unblocked. Please move your machine out of sight. It will give the wrong impression."

"Well I'm just plain Jack Brown from the city's cleansing department. I've been doing this job for twenty years and I've never managed to get this hose to stretch any further in all these years. If you want the job done it's here I stay."

"But you can't. What will the neighbours say?"

"Don't you worry about the neighbours. Would you believe me if I told you that I've been at all their houses – and do you know, they all say the same thing – What will the neighbours say? Now if you like I can park on the Lisburn Road but it would take me a long time to clear your drain using a couple of buckets. If you want the job done I'll be out of here in no time."

"Oh dear! Marianne run and fetch the deodorant. The smell will ruin the barbeque."

As Marianne dashed off, Jack sniffed the air as the smell of the barbeque wafted across the lawn. "Now that smell's just great – but go easy on the chilli and sauce or you'll have the same problem all over again with your drains."
"I didn't mean the smell from the barbeque. I mean the unpleasant odours from the sewers."
"If you were working with them every day you'd get used to them. My wife, Mrs Brown, was for divorcing me when I started; now there's not a word from her."
"I can't stand here chatting, my good man, I have a huge crowd of guests coming. Must fly."
"Tell me something before you go!"
"What is it and quickly?"
"Where's your septic tank?"
"Should one have one? Ask Marianne. I want you gone within the hour!"

Jack sauntered across the lawn. He could find the manholes and tank with his eyes closed. "Typical snob," he thought "hasn't a clue."
Marianne had given up trying to catch the poodles who were relishing their new found freedom and weren't going to give it up easily. She flopped down on the grass exhausted.
"I tell you what – I'll catch those two dogs if you sneak me one of the steaks I smell, and a couple of sausages."
"But that's going to take far too long and the guests will be arriving soon."
"Don't worry I'll be out of here before you can say Mrs Basildon-Blakely MBE - just wrap the steak up in a bit of side salad and put it in the cab of my lorry."

Jack set out methodically to couple up the lengths of hose and then engage the tanker pump. The poodles Madame Pompidou and Beau Brummel watched disdainfully from a distance, then frisked around as the work progressed.

Although it was a routine job, Jack made sure everything was in order before he began dismantling the equipment.
"Maybe you could test and see if the toilets are flushing," he shouted to the maid as he laid the sections of hose in the correct order. Marianne scurried across the gravel to carry out Jack's request, leaving the poodles frenziedly chasing each other in ever decreasing circles.

As he was replacing a section of hose on the lorry Jack heard a muffled yelp and turning round he saw the rear of Madame Pompidou jutting out from one of the pipes he had just used and Beau Brummel gyrating from the other end. Both poodles were in a state of convulsive excitement. Jack's eyes nearly popped out of his head as he watched them slowly disappear from view. Galvanised into action he managed to grab them in turn and yank them free.

The highly perfumed poodles were in a sorry, bedraggled state, their coiffured coats now dripping. In a panic Jack looked round wondering what to do but before he had time to think Mrs Basildon-Blakely stormed down the steps and made her way towards him.
"I instructed you to be gone within the hour."
"On my way."
"Madame Pompidou – Beau Brummel - come here!"

The poodles were partly released by Jack, partly freed themselves. He noticed that they were practically the same colour! Had her ladyship noticed? He did notice that she had changed into a pale blue evening dress. The poodles galloped towards her, obviously an old trick they had been taught. He stood transfixed as Madame Basildon-Blakely stood with open arms as the dogs leapt in unison. The look of joy turned to horror as the dogs snuggled on her chest and began licking her face, neck and arms. She stood frozen to the spot.
"It's working," Marianne shouted from the top steps.
"Good – I'll be off now – have a nice evening."

Jack climbed into his cab and ran his eye over the controls. The sweet smell of barbequed steak hit his nostrils. He unwrapped the steak which Marianne had left and eased his tanker into the driveway. His teeth sank into the juicy meat as he waited for traffic to ease.
"Maybe I'll have time for that trout after all," he mused

Malachy Falls

Malachy was born last of eleven children, to Peter and Margaret, into the family general store, pub and farm on the shores of Lough Neagh.

Some really wonderful people and characters called at the store; they made life colourful and enjoyable. He has some great memories!

He married Therese from Cookstown and they have four children and ten grandchildren. Malachy established a pharmacy in Cookstown and looked after the business for forty years until his son took over. He is now retired and enjoys a game of golf, sport, reading and music. He has always loved to read poetry, autobiographies, local folklore and listening to people talk about their work and life experiences.

Malachy likes to write short stories based on current affairs, or as a result of listening to people who called at his childhood home over the years. He feels he has a lot to learn but he really enjoys being part of the writers group.

His motto is: Carpe Diem - Seize the Day!

Late for Church

"De ye know, Robert John, we're on the last legs, as usual, for church. Was the car herd to start?"

"Not a bit, Martha, aftir two birls of the startin hanl away she went, even though the ingin was cowl."

The Watsons always looked forward to their Sunday worship. It was war time and with petrol rationing that was the only car journey, apart from a monthly trip to the market, that they were allowed. They loved surveying the scenery as they tootled along in their 1937 Austin 10.

"Boys, McMaster's barley is fulla ragweed, RJ. Ye'd wonder Sargant Patterson or the tillage constable hasn't been on their backs afore now!"

"That's nat lek them, Martha, everythin always has to be spic an span wi themens. I noticed the Harpers hiv a serious creamery cans out at the end of their loanin. Them Friesans a theirs must give an awful milk."

"Aye, right enough. Is the ingin missin a bit, RJ? Wud the petril be low?"

"Naw, Martha, I filled her yesterday. She shud be OK but she dis soun a bit funny. Maybe a wee bit durt in the carb or else shis aff a plug."

Suddenly the engine died. RJ got the starting handle, lifted the side bonnet back on its hinges and primed the carburettor. Then he cranked the engine with the starting handle. After several attempts, the engine gave the odd encouraging cough, but wouldn't come to life at all.

"We'll nivir mik it te church now, Martha. We may just walk home again. A'll lave her here and A'll git young McMaster te help me tow her home afore dark the morra."

Just as they were walking across the little stone bridge over Harper's Drain, their big five acre, market garden, hillfield came into view.

"RJ, look! There's kettle or big dogs on our hill. I ken see them!"

They hastened their steps and as they got closer RJ exclaimed, "Them's not kettle, Martha dear, them's childur; and what are they doin in our ground an it the Sabbath Day too?" RJ let a gulder out of him and both of them clapped their hands, hands that were well worn from weeding and thinning. Four or five children scooted out of the field and away with them up the road as fast as they could.

"That's them McCurdy skitters from up the road and they mist have been robbin our vegibles. RJ, ye wud need to have a word wi thir Da."

"Not on the Sabbath, Martha, but a will the morra marnin – him that nither works nor wants, ceptin tikin our vegibles, and hur so gran spoken!"

RJ and Martha entered the field to inspect the results of the trespass.

"Luk at that, Martha, thirs wee piles a carats and new spuds, an them not even near ready for liftin."

"An here's a pile a pays wi big, fat pods. Ye know, RJ, they wornt expectin us home frim church for another hour or two."

The Watsons were just finished their dinner when a timid knock set Jack, their collie, howling.

"Howl yer wheesht, Jack! Martha, will ye see who's there."

"Hello, Mrs Watson, can I have a little word with you and your husband?"

"Aye, a course, Mrs McCurdy, come on in. Robert John's in the front room and a'll put Jack out in the yerd."

"Mr and Mrs Watson. I've a terrible confession to make. Our children were in your field to-day while you were both at church and they pulled up a lot of vegetables. Worse than that, myself and my husband, Charles Senior, sent them on that sinful errand." Mrs McCurdy burst into tears. She sobbed, "My husband, Charles, is in very poor health; he has severe angina. He only gets five shillings a week benefits and we're all near starvation. That Sunday morning visit to your field keeps us alive. I am very sorry and feel so guilty and will have to make restitution to you and don't know how."

Martha interrupted, "Ye know, RJ and me, we're getting no younger. Sher we have neither chick nir chile. We cud be quare an glad iv a bit a help frim your weeins in the evenins and whiniver thirs no school. They'd earn a shillin or two, ans we'd give thim free vegibles as well. Is that awright wi ye, RJ?"

"Sounds soun te me, Martha. De ye know a cud be doin wi the help."

Mrs McCurdy cried with relief and gratitude as she parted at the door. "Mr and Mrs Watson, Charles and I will never forget you for this day. Thank you so much for the lovely soda farls and the potatoes you've just given me. The family will have a good dinner tonight."

"Martha, the fire's getting low; put a when a turf at the back. And whin ye're on yer fut, put thim two prayer books back on the mantel shelf. De ye know sumthin, Martha, the Gud Lord works in wunnerful ways: we learnt more the day about Christyin charity be not getting te church!"

Odd Job Bob

His father was Jack the blacksmith, known locally as Black Jack. The smithy was the farmers' gossip stop. As the sparks flew up the broad smithy chimney stack, so did the local chat and scandal ascend from the knot of waiting farmers. We envied the blacksmith's son, Bob, our school friend, as he had such an interesting father in a creative job – making shoes that fitted and gates that kissed.

Bob, or Odd Job Bob as we named him, often mitched school and the cruelty man was ever on his trail. But he, wily Bob, left no clue as to where he spent his missing days.

We often asked him, "What were you up to?"

"Just odd jobs!" he'd say, and throw back his head and laugh.

Then one day he didn't turn up for school, which wasn't surprising, but neither did he turn up for his tea, which was surprising! All and sundry searched for Odd Job Bob, for hours, it seemed. Then, when hopes were almost lost, Odd Job Bob was found cowering up an apple tree in a neighbour's orchard, with a Kerry Blue growling at the foot of the trunk.

Negotiations between Bob and the dog had broken down and welcome rescue came for Bob when the bemused owner of the Kerry Blue called him off, with half the parish looking on, gaping with glee. Odd Job Bob never mitched again.

Atishoo of Truth

Usually our morning papers contain something either thought provoking, or even mind boggling! This morning was a classic.

Latest directive from the Health Watchdog barking from its ethereal kennel way up yonder.

The headline read:

'***Don't sneeze into your hands no more; sneeze into your elbow***'

'For goodness sake!' as Stephen Nolan would say - the biggest blow in the country, sorry 'show'.

The watchdog barks, warning us against hand sneezing as a sure way of spreading millions of germs, be it on door knobs, telephones or the shaking of hands.

Is this directive serious and not to be sniffed at, I wondered?

On reflection, aren't there wonderful opportunities for the rag trade to boost their flagging sales in this time of credit crunch! Why not fit a sneeze piece in the elbow of every shirt, jacket or blouse, with matching colours for gents' ties or ladies' jewellery - or indeed manufacture slip on sneeze pieces in a riot of colours, in silk and cotton?

A new culture in sneeze trapping could develop, with differing techniques resembling perhaps the stance of boxing, with the southpaw, the crosscut, the uppercut the haymaker or perhaps the jab!

What happens to the tissue trade? Will the sale of Kleenex take a nosedive, and will the folk with the larger hooters no longer reach for the kitchen roll and dive for their elbow instead?

I was pondering what our Health Minister Michael at Stormont might think of all this, I was tempted to ring him, then decided not, as he may suggest that I stick it up my Gimpsey, and keep my nose out of his department. I really am undecided about this elbow sneezing, and can't decide whether to do it, or snot.

Who Wears the Trousers?

"Good afternoon. Lawson Accountants. Janet speaking. How may I help you?"

"Hi, Janet. Could you put me through to Cyril, please?"

"Oh hi, Mrs Lawson. The line's free. I'll put you through straight away.

"Hi, honey! It's me, Joan. My Mum's just off the phone. Her all-night minder can't make it tomorrow night, so I'll have to stay at her place."

"Oh, what a pity, Joan. That's the Rugby Charity Dinner night. We will just have to give it a bye."

"Cyril, those tickets were a hundred pounds each. That's a lot to lose. Why don't you go and give my ticket to your secretary, Janet. It would be a rare night out for her and it's really a must for you as a lot of our clients will be there too. Anyway, that's settled! I'm off to pick up the kids from elocution."

Joan was relaxed and comfortable with the idea of Janet accompanying her Cyril. Janet was an excellent secretary. With her school marm glasses, her pony tail, her face that never saw make-up – Cyril would be in good hands. Joan took Cyril's new linen look Armani suit from the wardrobe. "He'll look well in that," she thought as she ironed out a few creases.

The meal came and went. Both Cyril and Janet had good reports of the meal and of the friends and clients they had met.

"What did Janet wear to the dinner, Cyril?"

"She wore a long dress, I think."

"What colour was it?"

"It was green. Or ..... on second thoughts, it was blue."

"Oh, you men! I suppose I'll have to ask her myself when I'm next talking to her."

"Oh, Joan. The dry cleaners are delivering my suit to our house on Friday morning. They assure me they can remove the red wine stain."

Friday's free newspaper popped through the letterbox just as Joan was about to sip her morning coffee. She unfolded the paper and there on the front page was a large colour photo of her Cyril beside a beautiful girl in a long, flame red dress. Joan's cheeks coloured and crossly she thought, "Who's that with my Cyril? Must be a client."

She looked again. "By jingo! It's the dowdy Janet!" No school marm glasses or pony tail. Instead, beautiful auburn hair streamed over her shapely shoulders and the low cut of the off the shoulder gown enhanced a fine bosom.

"Blue ... no .... it was green!" Joan fumed. Then her eye spotted Cyril's finger curled round Janet's lithe thigh. The waist might have been acceptable, but the thigh was forbidden territory in Joan's eyes. And, speaking of eyes, those 'you're mine any time' eyes of Janet as she smiled up at her Cyril on the front page was too much.

"The cheek of them both! And on the front page! And in every house in the town!"

Just then the door bell chimed. Joan fanned her face and breathed deeply to regain her severely dented composure.

"Hi! I'm delivering your dry cleaning. Many thanks for your custom, Mrs Lawson," breezed the young lady on the doorstep. Joan thanked her and closed the door behind her.

Joan was heading for the bedroom to hang up Cyril's Armani when the front page caught her eye again.

"Humph! Green or blue! M.E.N. Men!" she fumed. She went straight to the kitchen and grabbed the long bladed scissors from the drawer With a few neat strokes she severed the trouser legs just above the knee.

"That will cut our Cyril down to size," she smirked with satisfaction, and proceeded to the wardrobe to hang up the suit.
When she returned to her now cooling coffee she glared at the offending picture. She heard a car in the drive.

"Bet that's Cyril home for lunch. The only meal he'll get from me today is hot tongue."

She went to the door with the front page in her hand. She opened the door. Cyril went to kiss her but it was refused a landing. Just then another car appeared in the drive. It was driven by the breezy young lady from the cleaners. She hopped out holding a suit aloft.

"Oh, Mrs Lawson! I got the names mixed up. This is your husband's suit. The one I delivered earlier was for a Mr Dawson down the road. SORRY!"

C.R.A.P.

Location, location, location – the buzz word in the property market.

Rotation, rotation, rotation - **the** buzz word as far as the new proposed requirements for the Northern Ireland DVA Driving Test.

Is it the steering? Yes and no. Is it the wheels? Yes and no. Is it the cam shaft? Yes and no. What is it then, that they have cooked up for the prospective DVA driving test candidate?

I certainly would never have guessed! It concentrates on the candidate's neck – rotation of the neck. The technical term is Cranial Rotation Assessment Programme – C.R.A.P.

The Agency has realised there is a major problem with drivers' neck rotation – and it's a unisex affliction as well. Perhaps you have noticed yourself, the need for the introduction of this CRAP.

Ever tried getting out of a minor road or street, which has no traffic lights, onto a busy thoroughfare? Picture the scene. The traffic is coming from your right as you try to emerge; not one driver turns a head to the left. Even if the traffic grinds to a halt, drivers still fail to turn their heads left. According to age and sex they look straight ahead or at the rear view mirror; they inspect their nails or talk to the front seat passenger from the corner of their mouths; they eye the talent or gaze at shop windows; they check their appearance in the vanity mirror and make adjustments. You will notice the front seat passengers – after sneaking a brief look at you, they suddenly also develop the same restricted rotational symptom.

Yes, it's a major problem, as the neck will only rotate through ninety degrees, (shall we call it the Stiff Neck Syndrome?) whereas CRAP requires an unrestricted one hundred and eighty degree turn in the new driving test. Northern Ireland is being used initially for this CRAP idea, and, if it proves successful. It will be rolled out across the British Isles.

A recent statement from the Minister of the Environment at Stormont reads: *I have no doubt that the introduction of CRAP will alleviate this widespread problem of restricted neck rotation; help eliminate traffic congestion; and improve road courtesy in general.*

The new legislation is to come into force on April 1st next.

Therese Falls

Therese was born in Cookstown to Owen and Kathleen Conway. She lived and grew up in William Street where they had a confectioner's shop. She liked that – they were never short of sweets or ice-cream!

Therese was employed by the Civil Service before she married Malachy, whom she brought to Cookstown. She now enjoys the company of her ten grandchildren, and looking after them.

Her hobbies are reading, dancing, walking, conversation, films and theatre. She appreciates having the local theatre, the Burnavon, on her doorstep. She very much enjoys being part of the Writers Group and looks forward to hearing the other writers' stories and poems.

The Wizard of Oz

Dorothy falls asleep by and by
And wakens up flying high in the sky.
Descends on a land ruled by witches
Lands safely, without any hitches.

Such a lovely place, but no camera to photo.
She's glad to be safe with her little dog, Toto.
Cinderella got fame from four mice and a pumpkin.
Dorothy has come to the aid of a Munchkin!

The witches they rule the Munchkins by fright
They plead with Dorothy for help in their plight.
"Oh, please go and see the Wizard of Oz.
He will make magic to help in our cause!"

"How do we find this wizard's abode?"
"Oh, just please follow the yellow brick road."

They sing, "We're off to see the wizard!"
As they walk through a storm and a blizzard.
The meet Scarecrow, the Tin Man, the Lion
Who are so pleased her help to rely on.

The Tin Man, he craves a heart;
Hopes the Wizard will have a spare part.
Their quest to the Wizard succeeds.
And they all get the parts that they need.

Onward they go and are all at their best.
They soon put paid to the Witch from the west.
But their search they did not cease
And soon they had captured the Witch from the east.

The Munchkins they sang, "Dorothy's our hero!
Hooray for reducing the witches to zero!"
Their land was now filled with joy and with laughter
It will be a happy place for ever after.

Plastered at Ten Years

Dad was reading, his favourite pastime, a detective story from Granny Sheehy's two penny library. I slipped past him, hiding his large shiny tailor's scissors in the Belfast Telegraph, tip-toeing my way to the bathroom.

My best friend and next door neighbour, Colette, was already in the bathroom. We secured the bolt on the door and I climbed quickly into the empty bath. Colette flicked the scissors in the air a few times, like a bird's beak catching flies, until she got the feel of them. White dust, like flour, filled the air in the small space, making us both cough and splutter, as she cut and cut with deft strokes.

"Sssh!" I said. "Listen at the door. I thought I heard a footstep."

She peeked out and the coast was clear. Mum was looking after the shop and Dad was content in his novel.

So back to the hacking. Large white lumps and dust fell onto the Belfast Telegraph under my feet as she eagerly continued. I looked down at her handiwork with satisfaction, looking forward to my release from months of captivity. Then came a sudden teeth-clenching screech of metal against metal. We both looked down in alarm and disappointment to see a large iron fitting which was scissor proof.

Colette panicked, dashed from the bathroom, down the stairs and to the safety of her own house. A few minutes later there were hurried footsteps on the stairs and a lot of loud talk.

"She's in the bathroom," I heard Colette's mum say. The door opened and parents and neighbours looked in, in shocked anticipation.
My Dad exclaimed,"Oh my God, so it's to the doctor in the morning to get her leg back in plaster of Paris!"

Got a Feelin'

Several years ago my sister and her husband were building an extension to their home. The builder was under pressure as the annual builders' break was imminent. The builder asked my sister would she ever be so kind as to nip down to the local bulders' supply yard to get a roll of felt. She readily agreed as it saved taking a tradesman from the site.

She parked her car at the builder's yard and entered the sales area, only to find a long queue of people waiting. There were four or five male sales assistants behind the counter so it wasn't too long till her turn came to place her order. She ventured, "I was sent here to get felt. Am I in the right department or do you do it down the yard?" There was a ripple of mirth both from the staff and the folk behind her in the queue and it was then, with extreme embarrassment, she realised the innuendo in what she had said.

The middle aged attendant shouted loudly for all to hear, "This lady wants felt so would some of you young lads take her up the yard; and when you're at it, make sure you give her a good roll as well!"

Sister, still red to the roots of her hair, hastily left with her purchase.

Next day the builder knocked to say they'd run out of felt again and asked her to pick up another roll. On the way she racked her brain for ways to avoid the mortification of the previous day. She had not disclosed her 'felt moment' to anyone. She tried deep, slow breathing to calm herself and to help her use the correct phraseology when she got to the counter, so as not to repeat the embarrassment of the day before.

She was still mulling over how she would broach the subject when suddenly it was her turn. She was still not completely sure of what she would say. She just blurted out a confession: "I made a fool of myself here yesterday. I came in and said I was sent here to get felt and believe it or not I want felt again!" it was a different assistant from the day before and he ventured, "Missus, you must be very fond of getting felt, and any of these cubs would be only too glad to oblige you!"

The five minute wait for the felt seemed like an age to sister and she left, vowing never to return to that counter again with a similar request.
She rang me recently to say that that very same builders' yard had closed due to the recession. She said, "I felt so sorry when I saw it boarded up."

There she goes again!

He Left his Mark

The work table was neat and tidy, as it always was; my father was just that type of man. Pop, as we called him, was a soft, cuddly man, of fair complexion, ever smiling and a pleasant man. We all loved him.
He drew the tape measure from his shoulders and consulted his note pad. Then he measured and marked the material with chalk, scratched his silvery hair and measured again. This time the chalk dug deeper and left a neat outline.

With long, slender, artistic fingers he checked the scissor blades, gave a little, satisfied cough and started to cut the material to his marking. The cloth pieces cut to his liking, he sighed, stood erect slowly and rubbed his stiff back as he moved to the sewing machine.

Foot rocking the pedal with well polished brown shoes, fingers guiding the material through the needle, he hummed his favourite songs. Soon finished, he slapped his ageing hands and broke into a whistle.
Pop always whistled when he was happy with a job well done.

Frances Higgins

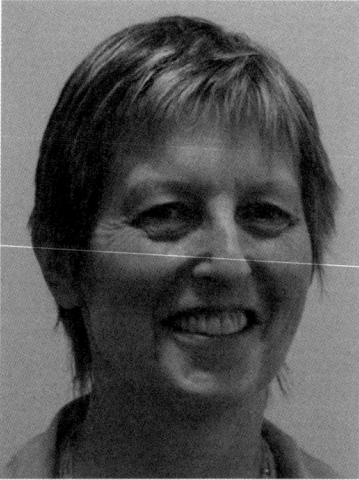

Frances is married to Eugene, whom she met in New York twenty five years ago. They have two sons, Stephen and John. Frances is employed by NEELB and works as a classroom assistant and First Aider.

Several months ago her friend introduced her to the Burnavon Writers Group. Attending the group has enriched her life. She enjoys writing stories which relate to her own experiences. Even more she enjoys listening to the stories and poems written by other members of the group, the laughter and the cup of tea!

Someone Like Me

I left my hometown on a bleak November morning. I felt the chill in the air as I fondly kissed my mother goodbye. I was seventeen, not long out of short trousers, a bit wet behind the ears.

My mother encouraged me to follow my dreams. "You're only on loan to me, son," she often reminded me. She worked diligently as a dressmaker, designing clothes to suit herself and her customers.

I put aside my fears as I proudly took that step into the unknown. Great Aunt Sarah met me at the docks. I was going to lodge with her while I did my apprenticeship. I can still remember the smell of mothballs and the pointed nose of a furry dead animal attached to the collar of her coat.

Sarah was kind and I owe her a debt of gratitude for providing me with an opportunity to further my ambitions. My hairdressing career was launched. My mind was open to new ideas. I was thirsty for knowledge and useful skills to empower me to lead a fulfilling life.

On my return home my dream became a reality. I opened my own business in the small town where I had been born. I introduced hair dryers, page-boy styles and, for the children, ringlets. Rollers and perms lost their appeal. The customers wanted innovation.

There wasn't a relationship crisis I didn't know about. I was sworn to secrecy on many occasions.

Then I met someone like me. Maggie Smith had her hair done twice weekly. I might add this was not for the benefit of the balding, grumpy sixty-something she had married twenty years previously! No.

All I can say is that with my experience and her listening skills we made a professional team and ran a profitable business for many years.

Things Happen

Have you no regard for human life? Do you have a problem? Are you sad, lonely, desperate for attention? Did you think for a moment what the consequences might be from your actions that night?

How are your wife and children feeling? How did they accept the news? Are your children teased at school? Are you ashamed of your actions? How is your conscience?

I suppose you would rather forget about the night you almost killed a young man with your selfish actions. He lay in the middle of the road after you knocked him down. You left him frightened and bewildered as you drove recklessly off. Fortunately a passer-by called for emergency services. His parents received the call that every parent dreads.

It still hurts, the thought of him lying unconscious in wet clothes. There were tyre marks on his white tee shirt. I tried to wash it clean as if I was trying to erase the memory of that night in October.

I still haven't thrown it out. And the tyre marks are still there.

View from Mount Sinai Hospital

As I look out the window I see yellow cabs hustling for business. Homeless people are lying in the street below, newspapers and cardboard boxes shielding them from the cold night air. The temperature in New York is sub zero. A man dressed in rags is waiting at the door of the local bakery; human kindness still prevails. I offered the same man a few coins last week. He politely refused. "I only take paper money!!"

Inside the building restless souls wander aimlessly.

What am I doing here? Where's my mother? (Margaret's mother has been dead for thirty years. She has no recollection of ever having children or grandchildren.) Who's that man? What's he doing in my house? I pay the rent.

Gerard brandishes his cane in the air and swears loudly. A confrontation follows. Staff intervene to calm the volatile situation.

Elsie

I'll cut the grass later. I'm off to the pub for a pint. Could you lend me a quid for a bet? McCoy's a sure thing at three thirty.

No, I didn't try that shirt on; sure it'll be all right. No I'm not going to your mother's this week. That woman should find a hobby. She does nothing but talk about her aches and pains. The Day Centre might find her a hobby.

Cancel the doctor's appointment! I'd rather see a vet. Sure he knows more; he doesn't ask his client any questions.

Go shopping on your own, love; those big stores put my head away. You'd be better shopping locally. You'd see far less food and spend less money. Have you heard about the fat cat salaries at those big stores? Sure it's scandalous!

I'll put the bins out when this match is over. Wee Rooney is just about to score; I'd put my bottom dollar on it. Coleen's pregnant with their first baby. That's another wee pro on the way. If he's anything like his dad he'll be good.

A week later down at the pub:

Arthur, there's a call for you. Elsie has been taken into hospital.
Sure I'll just finish this pint of black stuff; it's too good to waste. Elsie poisoned? How did that happen?

Maura Johnston

Maura Johnston has been writing for several years and is best known for her poetry.

She lives in Moneymore with her husband Kevin , also a writer, and they both share an avid interest in literature, local history and community projects.

Maura has delivered tuition in the art of creative writing to both adults and children on many occasions. She says she particularly enjoys the discipline and the camaraderie of the Burnavon Writers Group.

The Ballinderry

Camlough, that calm lough, fringed with reeds,
Lies secret in the quiet hills of Tyrone.
There, among the cobweb-crocheted whins, with
A sudden spring,
A sighing gurgle –
The river's begun.

Plaiting and purling, silkily sliding –
the water wanders along.
Tinkling and wrinkling, rumbling and tumbling –
this is the river's song.

Placid it passes through Dunamore, ranunculus
Drifting over the pearl-musselled gravel bed.
A heron hefts itself into the sky; an otter lithely
Insinuates itself into the tangled riverside weeds.

Plaiting and purling, silkily sliding –
the water wanders along.
Tinkling and wrinkling, rumbling and tumbling –
this is the river's song.

Wellbrook, and the weight of wheel and weir and years
Curls and whirls in the boulder buttoned flood
That, hiding speckled trout and snub nosed dollaghan,
Slips on past Cookstown, cradling salmon parr and smolt.

Plaiting and purling, silkily sliding –
the water wanders along.
Tinkling and wrinkling, rumbling and tumbling –
this is the river's song.

Below Big Bridge and Coagh Bridge fishermen cast and hope
And muse, as feather, leaf, twig drift lazily past,
Twirl into the merging dark Lissan Water,
Swirl as the river surges through Ballinderry,
Under the Footgo, into Lough Neagh at last.

Plaiting and purling, silkily sliding –
the water wanders along.
Tinkling and wrinkling, rumbling and tumbling –
this is the river's song.

For Patrick: 1947 – 2000

An evening seething with starlings:
Those uninhibited city birds,
At home here in the cut meadow,
Soared and swooped and scrabbled heavenwards.

You should have been here too, among friends,
Reminding us of other summers
That pulled the hayfield taut about
Twilight, funnelling the thran drum's thrum.

Instead, we talked of you, and how
You slipped away to open the field –
The skilled scytheman, whetting the stone,
Laying low the first untidy swathe

So that in the stinging aftergrass I stood,
An orphaned sister with a lost childhood.

For on a sunny September morning: fields warm, humming,
Dahlias vigilant in the garden;
Terrier for once not busy; house sound asleep;
You sighed, left your heart in Mowillian,
Were flung far from the farm, are a blind wanderer
Among ignorant stars where our thin cries
Sing sadly, wildly, calling you, calling you –
A startled stranger, a disarmed kerene.

Our heartache swells out at dusk, when sibilant springs
Whisper at muddy gaps. Seasons have
Congealed to the chill of horns held in thickets and
A scalded milking tin upended on the hedge.

To Catherine, Aged Thirteen Months

Like a boy racer proud of his possessions,
His own space, you tear up
And down the cot - pointing, babbling,
Watermelon smile splitting your face;

That smile that pulls my throat
Tight as the top of a bag
Of marbles. You poke your fingers
Through the bars, catch mine, laugh.

I hoist you out and you latch onto
My haunch and my heart, leaning
In to settle, a demanding little
Burden, fierce and unyielding,

Recalling old and weary weights:
A leather bag bursting with learning
Bowing my reluctant back;
The drudge and drag of bearing

Buckets of well water, lifting lumps of hay;
The stone of remorse that
Ground my sore soul into shards.
These I cast off, kicked, flattened

Into frisbees that bore all hurt away,
To leave lightness in their wake.
So tell me why, when we stop our play
And you go on your own sweet way

I suffer a strange and heavy emptiness,
Awe-full as worlds' woe, terrible in its loneliness?

To My Valentine as We Grow Older and Time Grows Shorter

When I hear the pock, pock of a snail shell
Knocked by a hopeful thrush upon a stone
Or see you trace the fluting of a bird bone,
I sense the hidden things that you don't tell:
Soul secrets, deep as water and as still.
I'll dowse for them, with wiles I've made my own,
And pull them to the surface one by one,
Caressing to alleviate their chill.
So come now, tell me soft that all is well;
We still can tread a measure eye to eye
And learn with certainty to read one sign
Of a finite eternity – the bell,
Flinging its tongue in brazen symmetry
Around the broken syllables of time.

Dreams in the Dry Season

The rain is a dancer
Tapping, tapping on the dirt road
That lilts to the town.

The town is a nosy hyena
Sniffing out secrets in dark alleys
That pincer the canal.

The canal is a calm hostess
Offering a sprinkle of sparkles
To the factory walls.

The walls are dawdling raconteurs
Entertaining the fawn grasses
That fret for the rain.

The rain is a dancer
Tapping, tapping on the dirt road
That lilts to the town.

So this is Spring?

So this is spring?
A deep lift of sky;
A flurry of light;
An awakening
Laden with birdsong.

So these are songs-
Tearing hungry holes;
Spiking the humdrum;
Falling through the air
Like shredded flowers.

So these are flowers –
Splashes of cold gold;
Twitches of purple;
Buttoning silence
And highlighting hope.

So this is hope –
As wide as the clean
Fresh fill of morning;
Sharp, clear clarion.
Sure – this must be spring!

Watchful

The rough peach stone
Lies on the window sill
Under the smother of cat
Who has withdrawn
For now
Her claws.
And when I touch her
She'll turn her head and
Look at me with eyes
As blank and stern
As any stone.

Gerry MacAuley

Gerry is a retired bank manager whose interests lie in reading & writing short stories and following the fortunes of Tyrone football team. He is also interested in golf.

He has four children and eight grandchildren, the youngest of whom takes up much of his time.

Gerry has been writing for four years. Much of his work is inspired by his grandchild and as a result he has developed a particular interest in children's stories

Gerry is a member of the Bardic Theatre Group and has taken part in *Affluence*, *One Flew Over the Cuckoo's Nest* and their latest production *The Field*.

.

Next Year's Turf

Sitting in the small barn attached to the cottage, Tom took the postcards from his pocket. They were his treasure chest and his dreams. He looked at the first one, dirtied over the years with his thumb marks. His sister never knew of their existence. The cards were from his first and only love, and he still loved her even though he hadn't heard her voice for over forty years.

He read the verse on the card:

In the gloaming, oh, my darling,
Think not bitterly of me.
It was best to leave you thus, dear,
Best for you and best for me.

His mind went back to that last meeting before she left for America. It was a sad, but cherished, memory and a small tear came to his eye.

"Tom! Tom!"

His reverie was shattered by his sister's voice. Quickly he returned the cards to his pocket and went out into the street.

"Right, Bridget, I'm here and I'll be going to the mountain now."

"Are you sure you're fit enough? Would you not wait until our nephews come to help?"

"No. I'm alright. The turf needs cut now while the weather lasts."

Head down, the old man pedalled fiercely into the slight headwind, the occasional spit of rain stinging his weathered face. The heavy turf spade on the bar didn't make things any easier and the brae he now faced was very steep, though he minded the day he wouldn't have noticed it. He struggled up the hill as far as he could, then had to dismount and then push the old bike up the rest of the way. He became very disgruntled, annoyed that his bones and joints were getting stiffer as the years passed.

The weather forecast had been good and he decided to make the most of it and make a start at cutting his turf bank for the next year. He looked at the sky. Aye, it was clear over Mullagharn mountain and the birds were flying high – a sure sign of a good day. He turned off onto a mountain lane. About three hundred yards up the lane was a long, white washed cottage. Attached to the side was a grey plastered barn and there were hens clucking outside the half door, pecking bits of corn off the street. He pushed the bike onto the street. The cottage door opened and out stepped a small, round woman with a coloured apron tied round her waist, her grey-streaked hair tied in a bun.

"Hello, Tom," she said, "You're bound for the mountain and you're blest with the weather."

"Aye, thank God. Everything OK with you?"

The countryside thought that they would have made a match, but he only saw her as a very good friend.

"Aye," she replied, "Would ye not wait until Benny or Dan could help you? You're not as young as you used to be."

"No, they've enough of their own to do and I'm as fit as my fiddle."

"Hold on a minute. I've something for Mossey up the road." And she went inside, returning with a big griddle scone in her hand. "Bring this soda bread up to Mossey. I promised him it."

Tom bade goodbye, took the bread and started off again up the mountain. She looked after him with caring eyes until he disappeared from sight, thinking, "There goes one thran man!"

Further up the mountain road Tom stopped at a small cottage at the side of which was a small garden filled with different vegetables in varying stages of growth. An old man was sitting on the window sill twiddling his thumbs. "How're you, Mossey? Alice sent this loaf up for you," said Tom, handing over the bread.

"Tom, you should have married that one. Look at all the good feeding you'd be getting."

"Hold your whisht, Mossey. Don't be daft. I'm looked after well enough."

He then took out his pipe and clenched it between his teeth and took out from his jacket pocket a pouch in which he kept tobacco. He reached in and took a plug and proceeded to peel slivers of tobacco into his palm with a stained penknife. When he had enough peeled he offered the plug and the knife to the old man. He rubbed the tobacco between his palms for quite a time, after which he took the pipe from his mouth, knocked out whatever ash was in it and started to pack it with fresh tobacco. Meanwhile the old man cut a slice of tobacco and did likewise. All the while not a word was spoken.

The pipe smoked, and a bit of gossip over, Tom continued up to the bog. The land was beginning to flatten out and the road got rougher.

He came to the end of the lane and left his bike at the gate which opened onto a well worn track up the mountain. He hoisted his bag over his shoulder and set off up to his bog. The wind had died down. As he walked he hummed the air of *The Old Bog Road* to himself, as was his wont on this steep weathered track.

As the track levelled out he stopped to take a breath. From the well worn pocket of his jacket he again took out his pipe and he proceeded to light it as he gazed at the beauty around him. Here he always felt a great serenity as he puffed, letting the smoke drift skyward. The silence of the mountain took over his very being. "Surely," he thought, "the beauty of the new bloom on the heather and the skylarks singing as they hover above their nests, prove there is a God in heaven. Time to get on, though."

He returned the pipe to his pocket and started onwards. He had expected to see some of his neighbours working their bog, but the mountain was devoid of any human other than himself.

"Well, I'll get more done. I've no one to keep me back," he muttered.

At his sector of bog he left his bag on a clump of heather, took off his tired jacket, lifted his turf spade and walked to the edge of the bank. Spitting on his hands he stooped and started to spade the turf sods up onto the bank. He worked with a steady rhythm and as straight a line of turf was laid as if done by a ruler. It was tiring and back breaking and after a steady hour's labouring he sat down for a break. The aches and pains seemed more severe than ever.

"It's much harder this year, and next year I'll have to get my nephews to help me," he mused, then wondered which of them would be willing to help. It was years since any of them had come to the bog with him. They were all mollycoddled by their mother, he maintained, and a day's work in the bog now would scare the wits out of them. More is the pity. They would never know the pleasure of standing on the mountain up above the countryside with its patchwork quilted fields as far as the eye could see and listening to pure silence. No, they would rather listen to that modern noisy music on their radios.

He looked out over the expanse of countryside below. Seeing the twists and turns of the road he had come up, he began to sing in his falsetto voice the one song he favoured most of all: *The Old Bog Road*. He reached over into the inside pocket of his coat and thought, "If only!"

His nephews came to the mountain that day but they didn't see the beauty. They found Tom lying on the heather as though sleeping, a serene look on his weathered face. Scattered around him were some postcards. One was held in a lifeless hand.

It read:

> *There's a sweet little lad that I wish I could kiss*
> *But there! What's the good of me wishing.*
> *In the corner you'll see a kiss, that's from me,*
> *But it's you I'd rather be kissing.'*

He had no more aches or pains to worry about. Next year's turf would wait.

Decisions

Sheila and Eve were having a heated debate. It had all started when they had been told a class mate had been assaulted by a man after the school formal dance. The debate centred around whether or not their class mate Jessica was likely to get pregnant and if so what would she do.

Both girls were in their last year of second level education and were most likely to gain sufficient grades to enable them to go to university. Sheila came from a fairly wealthy background, while Eve was the daughter of a farmer. Both were very strong willed and were on the school's very successful debating team.

"Well, " said Sheila, " if she is pregnant then I think the only option for her is to have an abortion."

"Oh, no! " replied Eve. " That would only make matters worse. I don't believe in abortion, no matter what. The child has a right to life."

"While I'm not really in favour of abortion. I think she should have the choice, and if she did take the option I would agree with it. After all, I dread to think what type of child it would turn out to be. God help her."

"Well, we will just have to differ on this one, Sheila. Let's not talk any more about it. What did you and Phil get up to last night?"

"Phil! Well, he has changed his mind about going over to Leeds University and has decided to try Queens with us."

"Oh oh! You have got him wrapped round your little finger!"

Sheila laughed. "Isn't that what we are supposed to do?"

The girls walked on toward the bus station, chatting about all sorts of things.

On arrival at the station Sheila said very thoughtfully. "I've been thinking about Jessica, and seriously, if she is pregnant she should have an abortion. If she doesn't, nothing or no good could come of it."

"Wait and see!" said Eve as she boarded her bus. "See you tomorrow." Sheila waved bye - bye and walked on homeward, thinking of Jessica's dilemma. She arrived home to find her mother in the kitchen baking some of her favourite buns.

Giving Mum a kiss, she put her books on the table and sat to have a chat.

"Any news? How was school today?" asked Mum.

"Oh, good enough," said Sheila "All the talk today was about poor Jessica."

"What about poor Jessica?"

"She was sexually assaulted after our dance on Saturday night last."

"Oh the poor thing. Is she alright?"

"We don't know. She wasn't in school today, nor won't be for a while. Eve and I have a difference of opinion about Jessica."

"What do you mean, a difference of opinion?"

"Eve says that if Jessica is pregnant she should have the child. I maintain that she should have an abortion, for nothing good can come of it."

"Why do you say that?"

"Who is the father, Mum? He could be a maniac! He must be - doing what he did. No, the more I think of it the more I'm convinced that all girls who are raped should have an abortion."

Mum sat down and looked at Sheila

"How can you be so sure that nothing good could come of it?"

"Oh, Mum, you are so old fashioned! I'm just sure."
"Let me tell you of a young girl who was raped. This girl lived on a farm, just like Eve, though it was maybe not as big. Every Friday evening, as regular as clockwork, she walked into the village and got the weekly shopping for her mother. One September evening she was walking back home when she was assaulted and raped. She was in an awful mess and terribly broken

when she arrived home. Her mother and father were greatly upset, but in spite of the police attempts, the culprit was never found. Like Jessica, she didn't know if she was pregnant. But after some time she realised she was. She had a very important decision to make. Should she go to England and have the baby aborted or should she let the pregnancy run its course? Her parents and herself debated the matter long into the night and she decided to have the baby, as she thought it to be a gift from God - and it was."

"How do you mean it was a gift? Some gift! What did it turn out like? Was there anything wrong with it?"

"Oh no the baby grew up in a family of love and the girl never ever regretted her decision.. Nor did I, for that girl was your grandmother and you wouldn't be here but for her making that decision."

My Favourite Uncle

The old man sits on an air-cushion in the high backed chair at the side of the fireplace, his favourite brown hat, a survivor of his farming days, firmly on his head. The priest is to call and uncle has been washed, shaved and his walrus moustache trimmed for the occasion. Worn and wrinkled his face may have been but his skin is softened with age. His beads slowly work their way through his gnarled fingers, his lips silently mouthing the prayers. Every so often he crosses himself. A spasm of coughing and he reaches into his pocket for a hanky. Blowing his nose, he wipes the tears that run from his sightless eyes. He leans forward.

"Is that him?" he asks for the umpteenth time

"No," is the reply, "he'll be along shortly."

He frowns, muttering about latecomers and, adjusting his hat, returns to his prayers.

The Call

The little dog barked, no, yapped, as Simon, passing the back garden of the house, walked up towards his caravan, which was one of many in the campsite. His head downcast and with a worried expression on his face, he looked neither right nor left as he passed the other mobile homes on the site. He had been down to the village, for his usual pint in the local hotel, which overlooked the tiny harbour and it was there he was handed the envelope with a phone number and a return ticket to Dublin enclosed. He felt it was vital that he return to his mobile home straight away. A young lad, whom he had never seen before, had given him the envelope. Finishing his pint with a long draught, he wiped his lips with the back of his hand, took his leave of the fellow drinkers and headed back.

His mind was in turmoil – who wanted to speak to him? What did anyone want of him? Why him?

He was retired for ten years now and all belonging to him were gone. He passed several acquaintances on the road but gave them no mind. Some thought it strange, as he was normally very affable and was always ready to stand and have a chat. Not today however. He opened the door to the mobile and entered. The inside of the mobile was quite spacious with a bedroom to the rear and a kitchen and living quarters toward the front. It was neat and tidy throughout and the seating, though clean, showed signs of wear. He sat down opened the envelope, took the ticket out and read the message again. Please phone 012 0349 8771 immediately. Intrigued he reached for his mobile phone.

At the same time Simon got the message, a meeting was taking place in a kitchen in Dublin.

Around the table sat an old man, two younger ones and a young teenage girl. The old man was speaking in a hushed tone.
"He should know about it," he said. "I found out he was up at his holiday home in Sligo and I took the liberty of sending him a return ticket and asked him to phone."
"Why?" said the younger of the two men.
"Because he should," said the old man, "If it wasn't for him, sure, none of us would be here."
"What do you mean, Granda?" said the wee girl.
"Well, "said the Granda settling back in the chair, "Here's the reason".
"Before we came here, your Granny and I lived in a wee house in the Sperrins, in Tyrone. Times were hard and I worked on the roads and your granny minded the house looking after your Da and your uncles. That wee house was thatched and there was no electricity or running water. For the

water we had to bring it in buckets from the well, which was about a hundred yards from the house, and for light we only had a Tilley oil lamp. There was no central heating like we have now, and if we wanted to have a bath we had to boil water on a wee range and fill a tin bath in the kitchen. In spite of these hardships we were very happy.

One night a young man called at the house. He was out hill walking and got lost in the fog. He asked for a glass of water. Your Granny brought him in, took the bucket and went out to the well to get the water. When she came in the young man, whose name, he said, was Simon, apologised for putting her to so much trouble and asked why she had taken so long, Had she no water in the house? Granny explained. He took the water and expressed his thanks. He stayed an hour or so until the mist lifted. Granny made Simon some tea and asked if he was alright to get back home. Simon took his leave and said such charity he had received deserved reward and he would not forget her kindness.

Two years later I was out of work. Your Da left to find work in England. Your uncle John was in hospital, and your Granny, finding things very difficult, was trying to make ends meet. Well one day she got a letter and in it was a sweepstake ticket with just six words on the note. 'Many thanks for the water. Simon'. That letter changed all our lives for it was a lucky ticket and we were able to leave the Sperrins and move here to Dublin. It was here where your father met your mother and your uncle and myself got work. We bought this house where you were born. Your Granny never forgot Simon and the chance he gave us. That's why he should be here. Your Granny always said he lifted us out of the rut and it's only right he should help carry Granny's coffin tomorrow."

Revenge

The teacher he did berate
Poor Sally for coming five minutes late.
Now for Sally it must be said
She liked to spend more time in bed.
Good timekeeping he said to her, quite stern,
Is most important that you learn.
She was made stand against the wall
For the school to see in assembly hall.
The message she did take to heart
And carried it through to her work.
As a traffic warden whom drivers fear
She kept all the town's streets clear.
She watched the times that cars did park
From early morning until dark.
 Only three minutes over would she permit
Before she'd issue a summons writ.
One day a Lexus shining bright
Overstayed five minutes. What a sight!
Now Sally could not let this go past her -
For the Lexus belonged to her schoolmaster!
A clamp Sally screwed to the wheel.
The Lexus now no one could steal.
Her teacher ran up out of breath,
His colouring the shade of death.
I'm only just five minutes late,
Please remove that bloody plate.
But Sally said with tongue in cheek,
It won't be off for at least a week.
And remember, Sir, what e'er you teach,
Always practice what you preach!

Goretti McCaughey

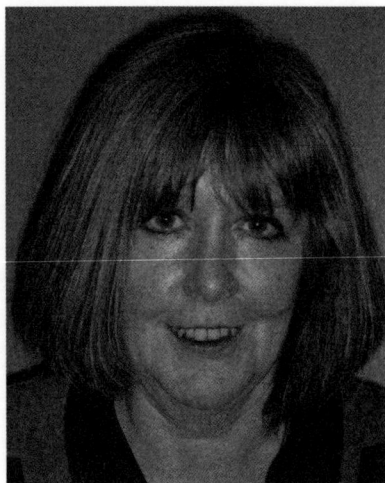

Goretti McCaughey has been a member of the Burnavon Writers Group since its formation. She works full-time in Dungannon Library and enjoys writing short stories and poetry.

Goretti has read one of her short stories on BBC Radio Ulster and has won a few prizes for her poetry in *The Charlie Donnelly Writing Competition*.

Goretti spends her leisure time reading, going to the theatre and being entertained by her grandchildren. She also loves travelling and in particular going on ski trips as often as she can.

The Bewitching Hour

I heard the wind kicking crunched leaves against the ground floor bedroom window as I dragged my bleary eyes towards the digital alarm clock. Four o'clock in the morning, I realized in despair and, worse than that, an uncomfortable feeling told me it was not the crackling leaves which had wakened me.

There…the sound of laughter… an eerie high pitched laughter. That was what had had penetrated my deep sleep. Then came a cry, "Mammy…I love"…more laughter…"Mammy..." I pulled the duvet over my head but chilly fingers of fear kept pawing my petrified body. Am I going mad? I thought, wishing now that I hadn't opened that second bottle of wine last evening.

"Nothing for it," I muttered out loud in an attempt to calm myself as I padded towards the shadowy curtains.

"Maameeeeee." My body froze as again the plaintive voice whimpered and again the insane laughter followed…

Apprehensively I plucked the curtain fabric an inch back and peered out from the side. An orange glow from the street lights gave a calming contrast to the storm's wrath. I could see the trees bending and twisting like break-dancers with the swirling copper shaded leaves their psychedelic stage.

Tentatively I stretched my head to take in the full view of the garden and driveway. No… There was nothing sinister out there. Surely no trick-or-treaters abroad at this hour and even in my hysterical state I could differentiate between the howl of the wind and the strange pitiful voice that I'd heard.

"Love…maameee"…laughter. The air shook with the sound. Grabbing my duvet I dashed to the living-room and turned the TV on, top volume.

When I opened my eyes again it was daylight. I must have fallen asleep and although all the fears of the night now seemed ridiculous I knew I hadn't been having nightmares. A hot shower and strong coffee worked its magic and I dismissed my fantasies as I donned my business suit and my business persona.

Still as I reversed my car down the driveway I glanced uncertainly around the garden. As I suspected the wind had invited in all sorts of gatecrashers such as plastic bags, take-away wrappers and newspapers. I was busy grumbling about the prospect of an evening tidying up when suddenly I spotted something disquieting behind a broken tree branch.

Goretti McCaughey **85**

My car snorted in indignation as I braked hard and nearly threw myself out of it. "Surely not…surely not," I gasped, getting closer to the limp, floppy shape. "Not a baby… I would have seen it last night. Please no… no… no…"

I reached my arm over the branch and picked up the soaked body, its clothes now a greyish white and its head covered in a little bonnet.

Now my laughter was as hysterical as the laughter I'd heard last night.

A doll – a doll with a battery –a battery which when beaten against a tree trunk by the wind had produced the strange sounds I'd heard last night.

I brought the poor little thing inside and placed it in the tumble dryer. "Someone might be missing her," I mused. "More work tonight."

Pay Back

That's what I'll do!

The idea struck Colette as she flung a pile of unsorted cutlery into the container at the bottom of the dishwasher and switched it on. Leaving the cups and plates dancing around the machine in tune with her furious mood she marched up to the bedroom.

Half an hour later she dragged four fully packed pieces of luggage down the stairs. The wheels tore at the carpet and the cases scratched the recently painted walls. Colette scarcely noticed and certainly didn't care. She heaved all her baggage into the back of her sporty jeep and sped towards the school, reaching it just as the home-time bell rang out.

Four young girls separated themselves from a mass of similarly dressed children pouring onto the pavement and jumped into the back seat of the vehicle.

Colette interrupted their excited chatter. "Girls, I have a surprise for you." Keeping her tone light she continued, "We're going on a little holiday."

Her daughters looked at the luggage with puzzled expressions on their faces.

"Shouldn't Daddy be here too?" Aislinn, her oldest daughter, sounded worried.

"Where are we going?" shrieked the other three in unison.

"You know that nice hotel in town with the swimming pool and a maze in the garden…well that's where we're going."

Not a sound came from the passenger seats as the girls received this news in stunned silence. Finally Fiona, the youngest in the family and one who had never been known to keep quiet so long, spluttered, "But…but it's only five minutes drive away from our house."

After that the comments and questions came thick and fast.

"We always use the pool without having to stay there. It only costs a few pounds."

"Did something happen to our house?"

"Did something happen to Dad?"

Colette took her foot off the accelerator. "Calm down girls," she answered. "We're going there for a few days and that's that."

After Colette and her daughters had retreated to their large luxurious family suite, all of them still smarting from the receptionist's curious glances, Aislinn took her mother to one side.

"You've had a row, haven't you?" hissed the disapproving daughter. "Is Granny fed up with us always going there?"

Unperturbed, Colette answered in a normal voice. "This is a better idea, you'll see."

When the children were dispatched happily to the swimming pool and, as Colette was blissfully aware, under the care of the professional lifeguards, she arranged dinner for five diners in the hotel's award winning restaurant. Then she rang room service and ordered a bottle of the hotel's finest red wine. While she waited she left a message on her husband's mobile phone answering service giving details of his family's whereabouts.

Some time later, after carefully returning the joint, husband-and-wife credit card to her purse, she sipped from the glass of wine and mulled contentedly over her decision.

"This time I won't have to slum it for days in my mother's overcrowded house while I wait for an apology," she sighed with satisfaction.

Baby's First Christmas

Sweet and spicy scents,
Twinkling fairy lights,
Tinkling melodies
With fires burning bright…
Baby's first Christmas,
Such a peaceful sight.
And… while snowflakes dance,
Painting her world white,
Baby's parents pray
For a *Silent Night.*

From Female to Female

She doesn't need to stretch her arms
To have us eating from her palms.
She doesn't need to raise her voice,
She's won in nature's random choice.
Oh lucky her… long may it last,
These little lives fly by so fast.
If only we, wisdom supposed,
Apologize before she grows
Into a world with our mistakes,
This Midas world which never wakes
To think or look outside the crowd…

Pride Before the Fall

"Don't worry," I yelled at the disappearing figure of my mum. "I'm all ready to take piles of photographs."

Thank goodness she didn't expect me to go as well, I thought. However someone had to be grounded enough to record her big moment. Shopping gives me enough adrenalin rushes, I had admitted to her earlier. But once my mother had seen the vertical water slide in Siam Park I knew she was not going to be content until she experienced it.

Ask rock climbers why they scale mountains and the answer invariably is simply because they're there.

A constant crowd circled around, some just to watch and some contemplating whether they should go up themselves I observed the optimistic daredevils, who were now having second thoughts, clamber back down the steps and I hoped they hadn't spooked my mother. No, I should have known that there was no fear of Mum chickening out.

A wave from the top was the signal to start focusing my camera. I felt a great swell of emotion as the tiny shape left the top of the vertical water slide. Her crossed arms reminded me of a corpse arranged in a coffin at a wake.

Click, click, click went my digital camera. Suddenly a great roar went up from the horde of spectators. Automatically still flashing the camera I could see what was causing the uproar.

"I don't believe it!" I cried out loud.

The force of the speed and water had wrenched mum's bikini top from her body. Helplessly she slid towards the bottom to the accompaniment of clapping and wolf-whistles. I have no shots of her standing up in triumph. Instead a bowed, abashed head appeared, then clawing hands as she swam to the edge of the pool.

There was still no elated smile…

She pointed frantically at the towels.

"Wait, smile for one more holiday snap," I giggled. "Dad's just going to love these!"

Awake

Dressed in a bright blue ski-jacket at a wake is bound to bring unwanted attention.

"Typical," I hear my friends say, "you never do dress appropriately."

"It's January and I'm cold," I protest but nobody hears me.

Still I'm proud that my family chose the jacket, a Christmas present, bought on the same day that I'd booked my *get away from it* all New Year skiing trip. I didn't foresee then that I'd be here at the head of this queue of milling mourners, and, worse than that, tonight the inner sanctum is out of bounds. Invited for drinks in the kitchen is always the best part of a wake. There, where emotions excuse all, anecdotes, alcohol and stories pour, the closer to the bone the better.

Meanwhile here I am boxed in between Bob the Bishop, so nicknamed for his power to spray prayers endlessly and alcoholic Alice with her seventy years of boozy breath bearing down on me.

"Doesn't she look great?" Alice slurs, keeping one eye on me while the other squints around the crowd for the next victim. My skin crawls as Felix the feeler creeps towards me. He hesitates when he sees the fixed look on my face. For once he admits defeat. No, there'll be no response from her tonight. Next comes wee Jack, towering above the crowd, moving them aside with just his smell. A tsunami of tears and nose spill flood the lines and pock-marks of his vacant, withered face.

"It's too bad... too bad... too bad..." His words bore on into eternity.

"I can't stand much more of this," I think.

These leaving dos are nightmares, especially when you find yourself the host of the most deadly party.

Seamus McErlean

Seamus has been a member of the Burnavon Writers Group for the past year. He describes the creative challenge of writing as therapeutic and a pleasant relief from the demands of his day job as a Social Worker.

Seamus lives in Magherafelt with his wife Katrina and their two children Caoimhe and Caolin.

Road Rage

"Move you stupid cow! Are you colour-blind or something?"

It was pointless; the elderly lady in the blue Ford Fiesta in front of him at the lights could not possibly hear him.

"What the hell are you waiting for?" he screamed, "A colour to match your outfit? Move for Christ's sake."

As the offending driver made her way through the junction and along the main street, his tirade continued. He thumped the steering wheel with the heel of his hand and his face reddened with rage as he spat out insult after insult. In an attempt to intimidate his victim, he drove his car to within inches of her rear bumper, but still she was unaware of his presence. When she sounded her horn and waved to greet her friend across the street, he demanded to know if she was "intent on driving or planning a coffee morning". He told her too, with every expletive he could muster, that this was a main thoroughfare, not a parking lot and that she ought to move her ass.

Further along the narrow street, she signalled her intention to turn right. While she waited for a suitable gap in the oncoming traffic, he demanded to know if she had been "born stupid or had had to work at it to be this good". After what seemed to him an age, but in reality was only a matter of seconds, the elderly lady gingerly crossed the road and parked in the space available outside the Post Office.

"About bloody time!" he roared, exasperated and shaking his fist wildly in her direction. She neither heard nor saw him as he passed and continued with his journey.

For the next three miles, he cursed and swore, a cacophony of foul language and spit. His mood was such that even the little things became sources of major annoyance. First the air from the ventilation system was too hot, then it was too cold. The low sun obscured his vision, the visor obscured it even more. The radio announcer irritated him. He aggressively poked the off button with his forefinger and ordered the broadcaster to "shut his stupid mouth". A farmer on a tractor, slowly exiting a field to get a better view, received his full wrath and a blast of the horn that continued until he was well out of sight.

He drove like a maniac; bloody farmers, stupid woman, that damned sun, everything, he felt, was conspiring against him. Eventually, tense and perspiring, he arrived at his destination where a welcoming party had gathered to meet him. A boy in a blazer and grey slacks motioned him towards the space in the car park that had been reserved for him.

Gathering his belongings, he stepped out and walked towards the assembled group.

"Good morning," he announced to all, as he clung to his red skull-cap that was in danger of blowing away in the stiff breeze.

"Good morning, your Eminence," the over rehearsed school children chorused.

The Infernal Combustion Engine

As the darkness of the late October evening rolled in, Paddy Joe began his nightly ritual of lighting the paraffin lamp. Not so much a necessity against the dark, for there was a fine flame from the fire in the hearth but, a welcoming beacon to his many neighbours who called on their frequent ceilis.

Gently and methodically he rotated the glass globe between his hands in front of the little pyramid of glowing turf. As the glass warmed slowly he took a sheet of old newspaper from behind his chair and used it to polish the globe, inside and out, the process repeated until the glass shone like the finest crystal before being fixed over the lighted wick and immediately transforming the atmosphere of the whitewashed room.

That taken care of, he closed the door of the small thatched cottage and turned to draw the blind on the window. Looking out to the road below, he watched as several cars passed, full of young people on their way to a dance in Carnaveen or Ballydrum. A few people passed on push bikes but times were changing, and pedal power was a thing of the past for most. The motor vehicle was taking over. It was progress, and he approved.

His mind drifted back to 1953 when he had been the first person in the entire parish to have a car, long before even the Schoolmaster or Doctor. Several years work in England, during and after the war, had made it possible for him to buy a 1942 Ford Prefect and in the years that followed, he had been hired to chauffeur couples to the church where they were married and afterwards to their honeymoon destination. He had taken the bereaved to funerals and on happier occasions had ferried others on day trips to the seaside and Giant's Causeway.

He recalled that he had not always been paid for his services. There were some whom he had taken to the church on their wedding day but all these years later, when their grown up children had flown the nest, there were expenses still outstanding. In the eyes of some, it was always good to indulge in a little luxury and to put on an impression of status and wealth even if the budget did not match the extravagance.

There was that time too, during the border campaign when the car was commandeered by the commanding officer of the local Flying Column to assist, as the officer described it, "in the war effort". Paddy Joe had been fit to be tied, so angry was he, but he was consoled two days later when the car was returned safe and sound with a bottle of Bushmills and an ounce of Warhorse in the glove compartment. No questions asked. No answers given.

His car had not always been so popular however, not initially, and that was due in no small measure to Bridget Philomena Anastasia McLoughlin, spinster of this parish, a woman who, in her own mind, never doubted for a moment but that she would go straight to heaven, while the more discerning observer regarded her as little more than an interfering old bitch.

On the first Sunday after he returned from England, Paddy Joe had driven to Mass. A miserable, wet day it was and as he pulled up near the chapel gate, he accidentally sent a puddle of water all over Bridget McLoughlin. By the time he had got out, ready to offer his most sincere apologies, Bridget was already en-route to the sacristy to report the atrocity to Father Bradley, a man in whom she confided all, and whom she kept abreast of any scandal or misdemeanour involving any and every parishioner regardless of its source or accuracy.

Her report to the parish priest lost nothing in the telling. Certain she was in the knowledge that he, Father Bartholomew Bradley, whom she regarded as a walking saint, would bring Paddy Joe to justice and make him see the error of his ways. She told him that Paddy Joe was only just home from that heathen country England and he had deliberately driven his new contraption towards her, intent on sending her to her maker. She had been lucky to escape with her life, and now she, a good Christian woman, was soaked to the skin.

That morning when the parish priest spoke to his congregation from the pulpit, in addition to his usual fire and brimstone, he condemned the sinful influences of England on the people of Ireland and left his terrified listeners in no doubt that the mechanised ways of the modern world were an anathema to civilisation and Godliness.

Paddy Joe never had a chance to apologise. He returned home that day a disturbed man, fearing that the next step would be excommunication while Bridget McLoughlin, as she did every Sunday, took the priest and his curate their dinner of potatoes, cabbage and boiled ham. No money ever changed hands, but a thank you from the old man and a promise to remember Biddie, as he called her, in his prayers was payment enough for a woman who regarded the act of feeding the clergy as her spiritual duty.

Bellies full and, if truth be told, glad to be rid of the incessant gabble from Biddie, the two men retired for the afternoon, the curate to the study where he read religious magazines while the older man ensconced himself in his familiar armchair at the fire, replete with a large glass of sherry and a copy of the Sunday Press or, as it was better known, the bible according to Saint Eamon De Valera.

As the afternoon wore on and the wind and rain lashed the parochial house, Father Bradley began to feel a sharp sensation across his chest and his stomach felt like lead. Perspiration broke on his forehead while his feet and hands were cold as ice. Fear gripped him as he believed that death was approaching. He tried to rise from his chair but as he did so, his legs left him and he fell to the floor writhing in agony. The commotion aroused the young man in the next room who ran to the aid of his distressed colleague. It was no easy task but, gently as he could, the curate got the sick man to his feet and oxtercogged him to his bed before racing off to fetch the local doctor.

Battling against the elements, on a rickety old bicycle, the curate prayed that his parish priest would make a full recovery. He prayed that he would get to Doctor McMahon on time. He prayed that the rain would stop and, he prayed that the chain wouldn't fall off the bike and send him over the handlebars into the muck.

By the time he got to Doctor McMahons, he was cold, wet and miserable and the doctor, an ex-army medic who had ended up in this impoverished backwater largely as a result of his fondness for alcohol, was none too pleased at the prospect of having to travel on a day like today when he too had nothing but a pushbike. Thinking on his feet, and allowing his pragmatism to overrule any clerical decree, McMahon dispatched a bemused, if not a little anxious, young priest off to seek the help of Paddy Joe McPeake and his Ford Prefect car.

Paddy Joe was at first, hesitant about offering any help, but the appearance, at the front door, of the saturated and forlorn curate, and his pleas on behalf of a dying man, pulled at Paddy Joe's heart strings and before long, all three men were bouncing back to the parochial house along the uneven road, the curate's bike tied on behind the car while he himself sat in the back seat snuffling and sneezing.

"Thank God you're here, Doctor, I'm dying," groaned the ashen faced elderly man as McMahon entered the bedroom but they needn't have feared, a brief examination by the old soldier and a few general enquiries about his dietary intake established the cause of the priest's condition; food poisoning, caused no doubt by Bridget McLoughlin's boiled ham.

It was three days before Father Bradley felt able to get out of bed and wander around in his dressing gown and slippers. The curate on the other hand, thanked God that he was vegetarian but, it was more than a week before he surfaced having taken to his bed that Sunday and lived on a cocktail of hot punch and Lough Derg soup.

It was a very different parish priest who mounted the pulpit the following Sunday. There was no hell and damnation in his sermon on this occasion, instead, Fr Bradley urged his congregation to, with the help and mercy of God, embrace change and modernity but, he added to be wary of those who would speak ill of others and of persons bearing gifts.

Driving Miss Daisy

Barney Gribben was surrounded by women. His wife had borne him six beautiful daughters and he loved them all dearly, but he had a special place in his heart for wee Molly.

Barney was a gentle giant whose children adored him. He was the centre of their world but always on the periphery. He could never fully be part of their little female conspiracies and intrigues. All of them, especially Molly, could wrap him round their little fingers and he knew it. Still he loved it and wouldn't have it any other way.

Every evening after supper, Molly would snuggle up on her father's knee and listen intently as he read stories from the large volume of bedtime favourites that Santa had brought the previous Christmas.

"Daddy?" she asked one evening when he was mid way through a tale about a little girl who lived in the jungle and had lots of animal friends.

"Yes love?" he replied.

"Could I have a pet?"

"Of course you can."

"Could I have any pet I wanted?"

"Anything."

"Even an elephant?"

"Yep, even an elephant," he laughed and continued with the story.

The story was not ended before Molly fell asleep on Barney's lap. Gathering her up in his arms, he carried her off to bed and tucked her up, warm and safe, beneath her Princess Belinda duvet. He thought little more about their fireside chat until a few days later when he arrived home from work and Molly met him at the front door, even more excited than usual.

"Daddy, Daddy, Daddy!" she squealed.

"Yes dear?"

"Remember you said I could have any pet I wanted?"

"Yes," said Barney cautiously.

"Even an elephant?"

"Yes, I did say an elephant," and he began to regret not having been more attentive in his responses.

"Well," said Molly, "I talked to Mammy and she said an elephant would be too big and eat too much so I decided to get a dog instead."

"Good," said Barney, noticeably relieved.

"Do you want to see it?" she asked, tugging at his arm.

The conspirators had been at work behind his back. He was silenced and could do nothing but allow himself to be dragged by his daughter through the hallway and kitchen of their home to the utility room to see a white curly poodle complete with basket, blanket, feeding bowl and pink collar. Molly jumped up and down with glee.

"Her name's Daisy," she told him.

"Oh, that's a pretty name," her father replied, all the while thinking that responsibility for cleaning Daisy's mess would fall to him, as would the feeding, walking and grooming, just as soon as the novelty wore off.

"We have to take her for a walk," said Molly, holding up the pink lead.

"Good," said Barney.

"In the park beside Granny's," said Molly.

"What?" said Barney.

"She wants to go for a walk in Granny's park. Then she can go and see Granny," continued Molly.

Barney had not quite expected this, but being the soft touch he was and seeing Molly so happy, he agreed to take them both, Daisy and Molly, the five mile journey by car, first to the park and then a further half mile to his mother's house.

It was to be the start of a trend.

"Daddy, Daisy would like an ice cream."

"There's ice cream in the fridge."

"That's too hard Daddy, Daisy likes the ice cream from Matt's garage."

Matt's garage was a few hundred yards away at the end of the street.

"Alright then, we'll take her for a walk to the garage."
"But Daddy, Daisy couldn't walk that far and she says she really wants Matt's ice cream."

Once again, Barney acquiesced and Molly and Daisy, like royalty on a state occasion, sat in the back of the car, all the way to the garage and back. It was the same with visits to the vet, the grooming salon and to Molly's friends. In no time at all, Daisy didn't walk anywhere beyond the confines of the back garden.

In Charlie McCartan's pub, where he always enjoyed a few pints on a Saturday night, Barney's friends bantered him good humouredly about the charmed life he led in a house full of women tending to his every need. Barney laughed and took it all in his stride. He wouldn't have wanted it any other way, but to counteract their humour, he told a tale of woe, painting a picture of torture and misery in a world of demanding, argumentative women.

"It's not easy," he would tell them. "I do what I'm told. My life's not my own. Even the dog's a bitch."

And the men in the bar always laughed, even though they would hear this stand-up routine many times in the future - and not believe a word of it.

Just by Chance

"Nothing ever happens just by chance!" declared Helen during coffee break one morning. "It's all in the stars…all marked out ahead of you from the very moment you're born."

Helen was a bit eccentric but since she was the boss, we sheepishly concurred that there may indeed be something in what she said and then agreed that she was an idiot as soon as she was out of earshot.

When she gushed into my office a few days later and told me that she was going to be married before the end of the year, I congratulated her and asked if I knew the lucky fella. "Doubt it," she replied, "I haven't met him myself yet."

I was flummoxed for want of an appropriate response and then heard myself blurt out "Good for you…that's the way to do it…Positive Mental Attitude."

"Attitude's got nothing to do with it!" she replied sharply, "I went to Madam Rose last night and she read my tea leaves. She told me that I was going to meet a tall, dark, handsome man and be married before the end of the year."

I had heard Helen mention Madam Rose before. She seemed to place great faith in the mystic's ability to see into the future despite the fact that Madam Rose had, at one time, been convicted of fraud and tax evasion. I couldn't help thinking to myself that if this quack had been any good, she should have seen that one coming.

"That's wonderful," I managed to say, convinced now more than ever that Helen really was an idiot. With the company profits falling as they were, I just prayed that she was not relying on this Gypsy Rose Lee, or whatever her name was, when it came to making really important fiscal decisions. I dismissed it all from my mind until one morning just before Christmas, an invitation arrived in the post. I was gobsmacked. It read:

"Nigel Campbell Farquhar and Helen Braithwaite Smythe request the pleasure of your company at an evening reception to celebrate the occasion of their wedding." And the date? Well, would you believe it? December 31st! I had hoped to see in the New Year in a drunken haze of Smithwicks ale, but discretion being the better part of valour, I did my duty and attended the reception. The bride, in a sort of lime green, certainly outshone the rest of her guests, and sure enough, there was the wedding ring on the third finger of left hand, competing to be noticed against the huge rock of a diamond that Nigel had given her on Christmas Day. Madam Rose's prediction had come true, Helen was married, and all before the chimes of Big Ben would welcome in 1974.

The visionary had been less accurate in other respects however. Helen's new husband fell far short in the tall, dark and handsome stakes. By no stretch of the imagination could he be said to be tall. In his brown and burgundy platform shoes, his head nestled between Helen's breasts when they danced, but she was a well endowed girl and that is perhaps where he wanted to be. If his hair had ever been dark, it was not in recent memory and as for handsome, well they do say that "beauty is in the eye of the beholder".

In his favour, and I'm not suggesting for one moment that it was the reason Helen married him, he had acquired a substantial fortune from importing coffee and tea bags. The implications of his success for Madam Rose's future were ominous. There is little to read in a tea bag.

There was speculation too that Helen might give up her job to join Nigel in the business. I lived in hope, but wouldn't count my chickens. Leave nothing to chance, that's what I say.

I spent the evening, engaging in small talk and danced with Sheila from Accounts. When I had been there long enough so as to be able to leave without appearing rude, (there's only so much Country and Western and the Birdie song that a man can take), I made my excuses, wished the happy couple well and headed for the door.

As I did, Helen ran after me and grabbed my arm. "Wait" she urged. "Before you go, take this" and she pressed a torn up beer mat into my hand. "That's Madam Rose's telephone number…you must give her a ring."

"Oh, thank you," I said with as much enthusiasm as I could muster, "I will."

That was five years ago and at breakfast this morning, I told my wife just how lucky she was to be married to me.

"Certainly not," she informed me. "It is you who's the lucky one, after all it was just by chance that I went to that wedding…I never really liked that Helen one."

And my wife.... oh, didn't I tell you? She's Sheila from Accounts.

Margaret McGarvey

Margaret was born in Ashbourne in Derbyshire and spent the first six years of her life in the market town of Uttoxeter in Staffordshire attending the school where her father was headmaster. The family moved to Stoke on Trent when her father got the headship of a secondary school. She has four brothers, one older and three younger than Margaret.

She attended Teacher Training College in Kent. A year after qualifying as a teacher Margaret married her childhood sweetheart and moved to Tyrone. They lived in Coalisland for fourteen years and Margaret continued to teach there until she took early retirement. She has a daughter and three sons and in the past seven years has managed to amass nine grandchildren.

Just by Chance

Rob had been dead a year now and Marie was beginning to come through the fog of grief she'd been plunged into by his sudden death. Every weekend one of her three sons came round to see if she was OK; to offer her advice and leave her angry when they had gone.

This weekend had been Paul's turn. Ma, you should do this. Ma, you should do that – on and on. As Paul's car pulled away from the door she angrily picked up her post from the hall table. She smiled wryly when she saw the Saga Cruises brochure. How she and Rob had smirked when they saw the big cruise ships coming into foreign ports. Not for them the luxury of big ships. They had back-packed across Cambodia and Vietnam; been on safari in South Africa; walked the Inca trail ...... and so much more.

That night as she sipped her large glass of New Zealand Marlborough, she picked up the brochure again. She was fascinated by the cross-section plan of all the decks. Why not? It was only a seven day cruise. Even if she hated it she could endure it for that long – wasn't there a well stocked library on board?

She knew the boys thought she was crazy.

"You'll go mad, Ma! It's not your scene at all!"

After her first night on board she was beginning to think the boys were right. Any decent titles in the library she had read and all the other passengers seemed to be in pairs or groups. The second morning she was having coffee on the deck when a shadow fell across her and a voice spoke her name. Looking up she said, "Pete!" Standing looking down at her was a guy she had known in her student days, one of the crowd – always dating the best looking girls – never her.

The next six days flew by. She couldn't believe they were already sailing into Southampton harbour. She and Pete had been inseparable for the entire voyage. They had breakfasted together, swum, danced, walked and drunk together. Each evening they had finished with a walk on the deck and then back to her suite and the king-sized bed. No, she had not forgotten Rob, but it was lovely to be with a man again.

As Marie prepared to disembark she saw Pete emerging from the direction of the executive suites. She had never been down to his cabin, probably one of those cramped indoor singles, she had thought. She beamed at Pete and he smiled pleasantly back. Then she saw the beautiful, blonde woman beside him – perfectly groomed, carrying nothing but her Gucci bag.

"Marie, this is my wife, Charlotte. At last she is over her sea sickness, just in time for us to disembark. Charlotte, this is my old college chum, Marie. I bumped into her just by chance. She stopped me getting too bored while you were sick, darling."

"Our car is at the dock, Marie," said Charlotte. "May we drop you somewhere?"

"No thanks," said Marie. "A young man is picking me up." Pete's right eyebrow lifted slightly.

"You look great, Ma," said Paul, after he had hugged her and bundled her luggage into the boot. "How was it?"

"It was exhilarating. I can't wait to book my next cruise."

Like Me

She was someone like me in some ways, but so different in others. That night, had we changed places as agreed, where would I be now? Paula and I always fell for the same guy. So, after nights when it stretched our friendship to the limit, we made a decision.

Whoever said, "Bags him; he's mine!" first went out with him first. And whoever had not said it got the friend. Then we'd swap. Two, possibly three, weeks later, on a double date, we would engineer a switchover, letting the guys think it was their decision, of course.

Then one night we said, "Bags him, he's mine!" at the same time. We glared at each other and marched over, each taking the one in front of us. Of course, two weeks later we did not want to change. Neither of us could understand what the other saw in her guy.

A year later I was engaged and Paula was planning a quick, quiet wedding before her baby arrived.

Now she lives in the south of France with her husband and her only child. A brief note comes each Christmas. Yes, it would be nice to catch up next summer in Nice. I try to imagine it as I put out the breakfast for my six before the military operation of getting them all off to school and me and him to work.

Yet once Paula was someone like me.

Love Story

I had been asked to provide a bed for the night for a young woman travelling through our land. I picked her up at the station. She carried just one small bag, and I drove her home. After we had finished our mugs of tea and apple tart we sat at either side of the log fire.

Her name was Misha and she had travelled from Belarus. I asked her if she had any brothers or sisters.

"I am the youngest of four." Her English was perfect; she had just graduated from the University of Minsk.

"I have two sisters. One is forty four and one is forty two. I have a brother of twenty four and I am twenty two."

"There is a big difference in age," I said.

"My sisters are from my father's first marriage," she answered, and then she began to tell me her story.

"My father, Aleg, was born at the end of the war. Times were hard and his mother could not look after him and so he stayed with his grandmother out in the country. But his grandmother often had to leave him alone. One day on her return she found him missing. For hours she searched in the deep snow in the fields around her house. When she found his frozen body she was sure he was dead. After many weeks he seemed to be himself again, but the cold had destroyed the nerves in his eyes and he was completely blind.

Aleg was put in an institution for the blind in Minsk and there he lived from he was five until he was put out into the world at eighteen. He began work in a factory. He had never lived on his own before and in a couple of months he married the girl who worked beside him. They were both eighteen.

They had two daughters, but after a year or so Aleg realised he had made a terrible mistake. His wife drank heavily and she neglected the two girls. Although there was no love left in the marriage, Aleg was a good man and stayed with his wife until the girls were eighteen and twenty. He cared for them and made sure they had a good education. When the younger was eighteen he divorced his wife, went to university himself and became an English professor."

Misha stopped for a moment and gazed into the fire.

"My mother, Olga," she said, "is a beautiful woman. She is a lawyer. She had many proposals of marriage but always said she had not met the love of her life. One day she was out with a friend when she saw my father in the distance. His clothes were untidy and his hair needed cutting, but all she saw was a tall, handsome man. She turned to her companion and said, 'He is there.'

'Who?' her friend asked.

'The love of my life,' she answered. Her friend introduced them, for she knew Aleg. Two months later they were married.

I was born around the time of Chernobyl and my mother saw so many babies who were not born as perfect as me. Four years ago my mother was diagnosed with cancer. My father never left her side all during the treatment. She is now well again. They are both retired now and hope to build a little home outside Minsk, leaving their twelfth floor, little, grey flat. They spend all their time together and when I look at them I know I am watching a love story."

Misha looked across at me and added, "I hope one day I will have my own love story."

Love Sonnet

In truth, I do not love thee with my eyes,
For they in you a hundred errors see;
But I do love you and you my love do spurn.
But, in spite of truth, I am pleased to love.
Nor my ears with your spoken word thrilled
Your gentle feelings to basics often prone,
Your taste, your smell. My desire is invited
To this sensual feast with you alone;
Tho' my cool wit or common sense cannot
Persuade my broken heart from loving you,
You leave untouched the longings of another.
I am your slave and will forever be;
But my heart I will never give again,
For, tho' I would sin, you only give me pain.

Brown Eyes

The phone rang as Anna came down the stairs – washing basket under her arm. She reached for it with her free hand.

"Hello."

"Hello, is that Anna O'Reilly?"

"Yes." She didn't recognise the voice.

"You probably don't remember me. I'm Matild Baird, we met on a coach trip to Seville many years ago."

"Of course" answered Anna, frantically trying to recall the person on the other end of the line.

"The thing is I'm in town for a couple of days and I thought we might meet up."

The next day as she drove into town Anna had a very clear picture in her mind of the person she was about to meet. After she had made arrangements to meet, she had searched through her old photos at the back of the cupboard. Yes, there was Anna smiling through chattering teeth in the Alhambra with the snow clad Sierras behind. Another showed her and her late husband, Fergal, under the arches of the Meseta in Cordoba. Oh yes, there was Matild, a big black woman, a social worker in the inner city, beside her stood Alex, her white husband - he was something to do with transport she recalled.

Matild greeted her warmly when she arrived at the cafe. They talked about the places they had visited together and especially the little restaurant in the back streets of Seville where they had all become a little tipsy after the beautiful food and the romantic music.

"My husband died last year," Matild suddenly burst out.

Anna reached for her hand and quietly whispered, "And so did mine."

"It can be very lonely" Anna went on. "I had no children and my family are far away but I keep busy with my job and friends. Did you have any children Matild?"

"Just one. I called him Fergal."

Anna stared intently.

"He was born the year after we met in Seville."

Matild took a photo from her purse and Anna took it from her.

The face of a beautiful brown boy looked back at her - and when she looked into his eyes she knew that they were Fergal' s eyes, her Fergal' s eyes.

Summer Time

It was dark. They met beside the gate at the bottom of the garden.
She had said "I won't come!" but there she was.

Every summer for the past three years they had met up and enjoyed their
holidays together. This year things had been different and their old pursuits
had seemed childish. There was an intensity in the air whenever they met.

Jack took her hand and led Kate through the gateway and on to the
woodland path. When they reached the lake he put down his old jumper that
he had had round his shoulders and they sat down.

They sat together and stared at the moon-lit lake. Neither spoke for a long
time. Locked in their own thoughts but acutely aware of each other. Then as
they spoke together they laughed and the tension was broken.

Soon they were talking non-stop about school, friends and the last six
weeks they had spent together.
"Remember the night we went to the pictures?"
"How could I forget it?" laughed Kate.
"I told Aunt May I was going with Tom - well it was Tom's bike I borrowed!"
"And Eileen lent me hers, Granddad just presumed she was going too!"

"At least Eileen's had brakes - I still bear the bruises!"
Kate chuckled as she pictured Jack upside down in the ditch at the bottom
of the brae.

"We were so hungry on the way home and bought that swiss roll and you
divided it in two with your rusty old penknife!"

"And we had to drink water from the stream to wash it down, it was so
stale!"

Neither mentioned how they had held hands in the cinema and kissed
quickly at the end of Kate's granddad's lane.

Jack turned away and looked at his watch.
"It's time we got back."
"Yes," said Kate
"Before we're missed."
"Okay.- let's go."
They walked slowly back to the gate where they were to part.
Jack kissed Kate as he leaned over to unlatch the gate.
"Until next year," he said.
"Yes," said Kate.

Nellie McGurk

Whilst Nellie has written a few short stories in her time with the group, it is mostly poetry that she contributes. She says, however, she feels that she has never actually written anything as it just "comes" to her.

She refers to her poems as her "visitors" and in describing them has coined a new word - "poemality". Just like people, each one has its own persona and aura: some serious, others spiritual, others humorous and some with a story to tell. She says that when any of these "visitors" knock on the door of her mind they are always very welcome, whatever their "poemality".

Socks

What is it with socks, they always get lost
Or is it only mine?
They're the very bane of my life – they are!
Disappearing all the time.
Ach!
They could wangle their way out of anything
And hide only dear knows where;
I could count on one hand the number of times
I've been able to find a pair!
So
With a look I use on leprechauns
I stared them through and through
But having to blink, now wouldn't you know
I'd one instead of two!
But
Lo and behold, Fate smiled on me
As I was given a gift:
A netted wash-bag for holding smalls,
Complete with a good strong zip.
So
Within this bag I captured the socks,
Defying with a witch-like scream -
"Get out of that, you so-and-sos!"
And I flung them in the machine!
Well
The cycle complete, I opened the door
The washing to retrieve
But as sure as Fate I near dropped dead
At a sight I could scarcely believe
For!
Like rascals caught in a treacherous act
Lurking within the seal
Were socks all led by a blue and brown
Colluding heel-to-heel
For!
The crafty oul sickeners had danced round the bag
Till the zip began to gape
And with a nod to the rest and a shake of the leg
They made their great escape!
Well
I didn't know whether to laugh or cry
At losing the war to the socks

As that cheeky blue one with its upturned toe
Just seemed to scoff and mock.
But
What could I do but give up the fight
And surrender in despair.
They're a curse and a nuisance and spirit-possessed,
Each one and every pair!
So
Don't weep for me when I am gone:
If you think of me, just laugh.
But on my headstone please put this
To be my epitaph:

"Here she lies at peace at last
All frantic searching o'er
'tis eternal rest for her
To be free of socks for evermore!

My Favourite Field
(Revisited after 46 years)

A field with a slight slope, in sunlight bathed
A once-proud owner relegated to mere trespasser
One whom there is none to chide, or even notice,
Standing still as a statue in this hauntingly lovely
uninhabited place.

A field fertile with a crop of memories:
Memories that infiltrate and arouse every sense
To the highest peak of fettered feeling;
Thoughts from the heart flit through the mind
As those sparrows now freely wing
Round yon neglected still-loved walls.

But all's not silent, No!
The age-old strains of Nature's symphony resound
In organ-drone of bee and flute of bird
And amidst this melody I hear a chord
Far sweeter, sweeter still
As beloved long-gone voices seem to speak:
Their gentle well-remembered tones reverberate
Within my very being.

In unseen arms I am embraced as they their
counsel give.
And yes! Oh yes! I listen well as tears come at last,
unhindered now
"Oh! Let them go," they say "Oh let them flow and
Give yourself relief! Open the flood-gates and purge
Your soul. Cry out, and cry it out once and for all:
There's none to hear so grab, with thanks, this rare and
Heaven-sent gift of privacy.
Surrender to grief and let it heal, heal, heal!

And when that well of grief runs dry
Please realise that life goes on:
That was then and this is now - 'a time, a place'
And just think too: 'tis part of
what you are - be glad!
But most of all remember this: - it is not lost,
You have it still
Immortalised in soul and mind

As is our love for you.
Now, raise your heart, give praise and
Please go forth
Relieved. Released. Renewed!"

With the softest "Thank you" floating
From my lips I sigh, then smile.
In moving on I stroke this ivy-clad post
And try to fathom why
All this that in my dreams appeared so real
Should now, conversely, seem
Like naught but a sweet, nostalgic
Atmospheric dream.

Fame and Infamy
(written for All-Ireland Poetry day 2009)

All-Ireland Poetry Day so let us all rejoice
As from Moore to Heaney praise we give
In united rapturous voice.

And for this great day I've a tale to tell:
You could hardly believe it's true
About an eedjit of a self-styled poet
In 1892.

Alfred, Lord Tennyson, had passed away –
Britain's Poet Laureate
And a Scotsman, William McGonagall
On an epic journey went.

O'er hill and dale and thistles and whins
He strode to Balmoral Castle
To the very Queen Victoria herself
For he had a thing to ask her!

Ach! You've guessed it – this silly aul fool
With a smile upon his face
Was sure the Queen would install him
In Alfred, Lord Tennyson's place.
But he was sent packing and Her Majesty
He didn't even get to see!
So back to Dundee he strode again
The whole of the sixty miles
With his head full of rhymes and his heart full of hope
As he jumped over streamlets and stiles.

And believe it or not, overseas he went
And strutted his stuff on the stage
But often got pelted with tomatoes and eggs
By people appalled and enraged!

But he said to himself, "What
Hallions they are
They know nothing; that's what I think.
And they hate me because I'm a decent man
Strongly opposed to the drink!"

So he kept strutting on like a cock on a dunghill

With a brain little more than a carbuncle
And all dressed in his kilt and full Scottish attire
He roared and recited from a heart full of fire.

And in truth he really was famous
If 'fame' it could be called.
For he is known far and wide
As the world's worst poet of all.
There's even a headstone erected
All in his memory
And his poems are still being printed
For anyone to see!

"This is Ireland's Day!" I hear you shout
"Are you stupid, or what are you on?
Doesn't matter what he was –
Give over! You twit about a Scottish poet
On this day, of all days, we don't want to know it:
Do you get it??!!"

Calm down, calm down, CALM DOWN!!
Quit your harassing and let me explain!
I'm not as stupid as I might seem
There's method in my madness as will soon be seen.
There's a valid point I'm trying to make –
Will ye gimme a break, for goodness sake!

And here let me say, to leave you content,
Though Scottish, he was of Irish descent.

And now as you've seen from this doggerel verse
I'm as bad as him, or worse!

Again, let me tell you, here's my point:
Who knows? In one hundred years from now,
Couldn't they all be blowing and bumming
About ME –IRELAND'S Worst Poet
This oul' Cookstown woman?

First Love

Oft had I thought of youth and bygone days,
Spring days of tiny flowers, enormous love
And you, my perfect prince of chivalry
Your sceptre, a slender blossoming branch,
Your crown, the sunlight on dark auburn hair!
How pure and sweet and innocent our love
By guilt unsullied rendered hard as steel,
Though seeming fragile as the dew-kissed web.

Years have passed and to-day we met again;
Two sparkling tears slid down still so-handsome face.
No! Not tears, but jewels, jewels, jewels
That I yearned to hold and keep and treasure :
A wish as futile as our precious love
That dare not span that so-called Great Divide.

Moving On

Janet came out of the shop and sat in the car to relax and regain her thoughts. Then she became aware of a large, silver Vectra parking beside her. She did not know the driver, yet was amazed to see him. This was the man she had met every morning for the past eight or nine months. He had begun to slow down as they went in opposite directions and always gave her a big smile and a cheery wave. Now here he was right beside her and doing the same!

Suddenly he came out and approached her. She screwed down the window, taking in his handsome appearance and good dress sense.

"Excuse me," he said. "You might recognise me although you don't really know me and I hope you don't mind if I speak to you for a few moments. I'm Jack Smythe, social worker – here's my ID. You and I meet nearly every morning."

"Oh yes! That's right," she laughingly replied. "Civil Service, that's me: Janet Leigh. Am I someone you think you know or have met before?" She was puzzled as to why he should acknowledge her at all, on the road or even now.

"No," he said, "it's not that. Let me explain – and I do hope you won't be offended. I somehow don't think you will, though. You see, with the experience of my job I've become quite good at weighing people up and that's why I feel so sure you will understand. The truth is, it's this car I've been waving at. It used to be mine and I just loved it. I have such happy, happy memories of it, especially when Mum was living. Wonderful days out as she sat beside me there in that very seat. People are always talking about 'moving on', but I'm one of those people who finds it very hard – sentimental old fool, that's me!"

"No, not in the least," said Janet emphatically. "I know exactly what you mean. I'm the very same and I wouldn't like to part with Bluebell either." "Did you say Bluebell? I don't believe it!" he exclaimed. "That's what I called her too. Ach! It must have been nice for her to go to someone who already knew her name!"

They both burst out laughing together at this childlike humour. Then Janet, to her own surprise, found herself asking him if he would like to get in and sit in Mum's seat for a few moments, just for old time's sake. No sooner asked than done! He literally jumped at the chance.

"Oh, thank you. Wasn't I spot-on in my assessment of you? You are so kind but please, please, for your own safety, don't ever again be so accommodating to a complete stranger."

"Oh no, I won't," she affirmed. As time flew, she found herself becoming more and more attracted to this lovely man. They discovered just how much they had in common; realised they could indeed be soul-mates. She could almost hear the ping of Cupid's arrows on the windscreen. "Thank you, Bluebell," she breathed inwardly, "Please let this be the start of something good for me at last. Bluebell, it will be you who brought us together. "She talked to the car as though it were a person.

She watched as he gently and lovingly started to stroke the dashboard. He seemed to have gone into a world of his own and she instinctively knew not to speak. Suddenly he came back to reality and, turning round in the seat to look her straight in the eyes said, "Thank you, thank you, you are the most understanding person I have ever had the pleasure to meet. I can't begin to tell you what you have done for me this day. I hope it will be the first therapeutic step in my moving on – thanks again to you!"

Her heart began to thump in his presence. She found herself warming to him more and more with each passing moment.

"Goodness gracious!" he exclaimed in a now-down-to-earth tone. "I really must go. I've lost track of time, I've been enjoying myself so much." Reaching out he touched her arm for a fleeting moment. His gaze fell on her naked finger. "No rings?" he enquired in surprise. "There's some man out there who doesn't know just how lucky he's going to be. You are a lovely, lovely girl in every way and I wish you all the very best. I only hope he will be worthy of you!"

He paused, then continued, "My wife couldn't understand why I didn't want to change this car. Maybe there are things about me that are hard to understand. She is a great wife and mother and dear bless her, I must say she was always more than happy to sit in the back with our two girls and let Mum have this front seat."

Poor Janet felt like a balloon that had been assaulted by a darning needle; she felt completely deflated. Gripping the steering wheel with both hands, she smiled bravely as he thanked her once more and departed.

"Poor wee silly, silly, romantic me," she thought as tears slid down her cheeks.

'Move on, move on, move on!' thumped the rhythm of her heart.
"Yes, move on, move on," echoed her mind.
"That's exactly what I have to do, Bluebell, and so have you. I just feel the relationship between you and me has just been ruined! Sorry, Bluebell, sorry, sorry!"

Wiping her tears, she started the engine and headed straight for the trade-in department of her garage.

Rosealeen McKeown

Rosealeen McKeown is a retired nurse and midwife. Following enforced early retirement due to a major heath crisis, she qualified in Counselling and Adult Education and has worked in both sectors in a voluntary capacity.

She has written poems and short stories since primary school days and is currently completing her first play.

The Wraith

(accepted for BBC Radio Ulster's My Story: April 2005)

If anyone had ever asked me if I would be frightened to see a ghost I know what I would have replied – scared witless! Of course you would have to realise what it was you were seeing and so, when it happened to me, I wasn't the least bit scared as I didn't know I was looking at a ghost.

This is how it happened. When I was a small girl growing up in our one-and-a half-street village it was impossible not to know and be known by everyone. Across the street from us was a tall old house with long, narrow windows and a drab grey front. The grim appearance was completed by a flight of stone steps leading up to a heavy, dark brown door – the hall door as it was called in those days. This was usually kept firmly closed to denote the higher social status of its owners.

It was here that a pleasant old gentleman lived with a not-so-pleasant housekeeper who looked after him. He was not out very much in his last years but could often be seen sitting at one of the downstairs windows reading or sometimes just watching the world go by as the village went about its daily routine. Traffic was practically non-existent at that time and we children were free to play on the footpaths or in the middle of the road, as we pleased. During our games we would often catch the old gentleman looking out at us, his book resting on his knee. When this happened we would wave gaily up to him and he would smile warmly and courteously return the wave.

Well, the summer passed quickly, as such good days will, especially during school holidays, and in the hurly burly of schoolbags and new shoes, some time had passed before I missed him at the window. When I asked my mother she told me he had suffered a severe stroke and was now confined to his bedroom all the time. I had no idea, of course, what a stroke meant, or how it would affect a person, and so I was completely unaware that he would be unable to leave his bed ever again.

At that time we had a weekly film show in the village hall, and since the parents in general judged it to be over at a reasonable hour, most of the local children were allowed to go. It was on one of these nights, on the way back home that it happened. It was a clear, warm, moonlit night as we all straggled along, in no hurry to get home. There was a lively debate going on about the movie, and anyway home was only just around the corner.

I was slightly behind the others and just passing the tall house when I suddenly felt drawn to look upwards. There was the old gentleman standing upright and alone at one of the front windows – his bedroom I supposed – the net curtain held slightly aside in his hand. I was so happy to see him, and to think that he was better, that, without thinking, my hand automatically gave him our familiar wave. This was returned in the usual courteous manner, though I recalled afterwards that he had not smiled.

Bursting into our kitchen I excitedly relayed the good news to my mother who questioned me in great detail to make sure I had not imagined the whole thing or, even worse, made it all up, as I was known to be a fanciful child. Satisfied at last, she exchanged a strange look with my father, but nothing more was said about it. Supper was served and we were hustled off to bed in readiness for another school day.

The sad news came the next morning. The old gentleman had passed away during the night. It was years later that my mother explained to me about his condition and how he hadn't been able to leave his bed since the stroke. Granny said that what I had seen was his wraith shortly before he died. But they hadn't told me at the time as they thought it would be too frightening for me.

Many a time over the years I've thought of him and am still glad I saw him that night for the last time; even though a little shiver runs down my spine. How could I not be glad? After all, it was just his way of saying goodbye to his village and to me.

A Letter to America
Or 'Blown on the Wind'

Dear Seamus,

When I started this letter I remember thinking how surprised you would be to hear from me after all these years. Somehow we lost touch and time has a way of flying by unnoticed, hasn't it? Unforeseen events have overtaken us, and now it will always be one of my lifelong regrets that you will never actually get to read this letter.

How I recall the first time we met, or rather the first time we set eyes on each other at Sunday Mass in our little village chapel of all places, both of us in the bosom of our families. You must have been there lots of times before, probably every week - how did I not notice you? Must be I hadn't graduated into looking at boys yet, so that's how you came to be my first magical experience.

Sitting across the aisle from each other, that fateful morning, we connected instantly, our thoughts like a bridge between us. You with your mischievous blue eyes and your golden head, the slanting sun coming through the chapel window and resting on it like a benediction; your mother, a large daunting woman soon caught onto our silent communication and dunted you fiercely into line with her elbow. My mother, too absorbed in her prayers, took no notice of us, or there would have been a lot more dunting delivered.

We watched out for each other after that and Sunday quickly became the high spot of the week; strange how a relationship could grow between us, seeing as we had no other contact, you being in the country and me in the village. But destiny would have her way and she took a hand in the affair in the form of St. Patrick's Day. As luck would have it Ballydrean was to be one of the main centres of the celebrations.

The village folk, never slow to see the advantages of this, set about turning every possible establishment into an eating house as they were called then. Even the humblest cottage advertised itself as providing 'Irish Stew, Ham, Teas, etc'. Of course, all the young girls including yours truly became waitresses overnight. Excitement was high until finally the great day arrived - March the Seventeenth.

The village was a hive of activity, bands paraded, speeches were thundering through the loudspeakers but the waitresses saw little of this. We were kept on the hop by the matriarchs of the eating house. Tables to be laid, bread buttered and great vats of stew to be re-heated before the mobs descended on us.

It was early afternoon when you came in with your father and sat down in the corner to order your dinners. Needless to say I quickly made myself your waitress. Of course, I'd taken great care with my appearance in the hope of seeing you and when I did, I thought how lucky it was that you found the right place. Chance was not involved though, for unknown to me you had checked out all the other places, and finally found me. You managed to get me alone long enough to make a date for the fun fair that night, when all the eating would be over and the men retired to the pubs for the night. My first date with you, how marvellous was that! I was walking on air.

Walking on air, I was flying through the air up in the swing boats so high I could have pulled leaves off the nearby trees. The common, so ordinary looking by day, was now transformed for a few nights into a wonderland, and us along with it. Lights and music were everywhere! Rushing from one ride to another, strolling hand in hand, wishing the night would never end.

The fun fair closed down at midnight and we parted company on the village street, at the pub where you were to meet your father and uncles.

Thus began our long and sweetly innocent love story. Cycling the country lanes, walking for miles on the summer evenings, sitting contentedly by the river; weekends we went on excursions to the seaside, Donegal mostly - or we stayed at home to dance to the show bands or watch the weekly film show in the village hall. Walking down an orchard yesterday, you were with me - remember Seamus the apple pulling; pushing and shoving and laughing, teasing and whispering in this very lane. Happy days! Could it be that it was all so simple then? The faces, - so young and fresh; not yet written on by life's experiences.

How soon it was all to come to an end. An end in the form of your uncle home on holiday from the States- Yankee Pat as they called him; fairly turned your head with wonderful yarns of life in New York. Oh, by the time he had finished telling you of that wonderful world out there, you were seeing streets paved with gold. Between that, and pressure from your parents, the rest was easy. To be fair, your mother and father had nine other children to think about and surely your uncle's invitation must have seemed heaven sent. It was a done deal, so you decided to go back with Yankee Pat.

The night you told me, our last night together, I thought my heart would break. Well, maybe that's what did happen. I didn't know then, and I don't know now. I guess I'll never know. All I remember is the desperate sinking feeling as you tried so hard to gently and quietly explain, to justify your decision to make me understand. How could there be any understanding of it, me here and you thousands of miles away across the Atlantic Ocean? I'd often read in books where one of the characters on the receiving end of bad news 'felt an icy hand grip their heart'; without really knowing what it meant. Well, I found out that night.

Oh, there were the solemn promises to write often, maybe even visit, but I think we both knew deep down that it would never come to pass. What did come to pass was that our lives that were once so entwined lived separately and far apart. Time took care of the rest; the years flew by uneventfully, for me anyway. I heard from someone that you were a grandfather, so I guess that you must have married out there.

The letter from your cousin came last week; it was good of her to contact all of the old crowd and let us know you had passed away. Not that there's many of us left now in the old country, all scattered like chaff to the four corners of the earth. So here I am Seamus, in Donegal for the weekend, standing at your favourite spot, in fact; remember St. John's Point? And this letter in my hand, soon to be ashes, waiting to be cast into the ocean. Is it not a fitting memorial to you?

Nothing between us now Seamus but the vast Atlantic, when there used to be so much more. The sun has just appeared, hitting the steely water to form a shining ribbon, a pathway from me to you. You would think the Almighty had looked down and recognised the importance of the occasion. I wonder are you watching now as all these memories, sad and happy, leave my hand to go towards you wherever in America you are now resting. Feeling the salty breeze in my face, I turn to the sun, open my clasped hands and set them free; free to be blown on the wind.

The Dancing Queen

Slowly she pirouettes,
Slowly and gracefully,
Feathers in her foot steps
Stones where her heart should be.

Nobody knows her sorrow.
Nobody knows her pain.
Perhaps she sometimes wonders
If she'll ever smile again.

Keeping time to the music
Turning her regal head,
Her body alive with motion
But inside her soul is dead.

How will her story end
When it comes to the final scene
With her secret still unknown?
The dancing, dancing queen.

On Sin (and......temporary loss of faith)

A corridor of empty years,
A footstep echoes low,
And close behind me treads
No matter where I go.......
Reflection in a passing glance
Familiar to my eyes,
But with the inner soul unclad,
No merciful disguise.
Useless to avoid this sight
Ghastly though it be –
Painful, dreadful are the scars
Of lost humanity.

And I am not alone in this,
Thousands here do stray
Upon the sordid cobblestones
Of sweetness in decay

Of principles now dead and gone
Or seen in other light;
Of faith lost in the dark despair
And hopelessness of night.

Of faith lost in the darkest pit –
Where only God can save.
But who would DARE
To face him there?
Only the brave!

Moving On

Amy rubbed her eyes wearily and turned over in bed to peer at the bedside clock. Twenty past one in the morning and she was still wide awake. Sleep wouldn't come, she knew that from experience, not till Jim rolled in fresh from his latest conquest. I should leave him and be done with it, she thought, but dismissed this outright with the reassuring thought that he always came home to her. Only this night he didn't. Maybe a cup of Horlicks and a sleeping pill would help. Pulling on her robe and slippers she made her way downstairs in the empty house. It felt as if she were the only person in the world awake. The street outside was quiet; no sight or sound of Jim's car. Sleep came in fits and starts and Amy was glad to see the morning light.

No word from Jim, and the clock now showed eight thirty. He'd be in the hospital by now, ready to start his rounds. Well she wasn't going to ring about him; she must preserve some pride, some shred of dignity. No, she would let the day take its normal course and wait to see what developed in the evening.

It was almost six when she heard his car in the drive and his feet in the tiled hallway. One look at his face, tense and paler than usual, told her something major was about to happen. Even then she was totally unprepared for his first words. There was no greeting, no preamble, just a bald statement that he had obviously been practising all day.

Amy stared at her husband in stunned disbelief.

"Moving on? And what exactly do you mean by 'moving on'?" She'd always been used to his philandering ways, even accepting of them, after all it was always her he came back to.

Looking at the grim set of his jaw, she realised this was something different. This was serious stuff. How was she going to get her head round this? She would be the talk of the village; that pathetic figure, the deserted wife. In modern language, she was dumped.

Jim sighed in exasperation as though he were the injured party and replied in clipped, icy tones, "It means exactly what it says. I'm leaving you, getting out of this suffocating marriage before it saps any bit of life that's left in me. It's kinder and best to say it out plain. There's no easy way to do these things."

Amy looked at her husband of ten years, trying to imagine life without him. She'd be an object of pity. There'd be snide remarks, behind-backs conversations that would suddenly cease when she entered a room. Oh, how was she going to bear it?

She took a deep, calming breath, trying to control the rage inside her.

"I take it this latest affair isn't one of your usual flings, or you wouldn't be leaving home. You've always been far too fond of your creature comforts for that. So who is it this time- your secretary the tenth time around or the new nurse in ICU?"

Jim spread his hands in a gesture of appeal.

"It doesn't really matter, does it? Let's try and be civilised about this. Tell you what, why don't you make us our usual cocktail; one last drink for old times sake? I'll just go and pack a few things and get the rest later."

This last came back over his shoulder as he tripped lightly up the stairs. Even his footsteps seemed carefree and callous. Amy nodded slowly and thoughtfully in response. Yes, she could do that. Why not? After all, surely ten years of marriage warranted that, one last drink together.

Various thoughts flitted through her mind as she opened the drinks cabinet and cast her eye over the glasses inside. There was Jim's favourite, a Waterford crystal embellished with a tiny gold harp. Yes, that would do very nicely. It would be kind of symbolic for his farewell. It would help to tell the two glasses apart. This was vital. There must be no mistake. She couldn't have him getting the wrong one. With a heavy heart she mixed the drinks in the cocktail shaker, pouring them out carefully in equal amounts.

Reaching for her handbag she rooted round in it till her fingers found the smooth plastic of the bottle of sleeping pills, pills that Jim had prescribed for her when she was having a spell of restless nights. Little did he know then what purpose they would serve. Depression began to settle on her shoulders like a black, leaden cloak. Jim's feet moved back and forth upstairs as he opened and closed drawers and wardrobes. The sounds of his packing were so final now.

Amy turned back to the drinks cabinet again and, deftly opening each capsule, tipped the powder from them into one of the glasses, watching almost dreamily as the powder descended in a spiral through the sparkling liquid, to dissolve and disappear completely at the bottom. A heavy sigh escaped her. There! It was done! There was no other solution, and anyway it was too late to turn back now. She could hear his feet on the stairs, not so light this time with two heavy bags to manage.

Jim dropped his luggage in the hall and, coming into the sitting room, headed, favourite glass in hand, towards the armchairs where they always sat. Amy picked up her own glass and sat down opposite him at the small, oak coffee table. Heart thumping, she began to sip, watching Jim carefully and saying nothing. Two swallows and his drink was gone. Oh, he couldn't wait to get away and to be moving on.

Oh yes, my darling, you'll be moving on all right, only just not quite the way you planned!

The Coach

They say it comes All Hallow's Eve
Along the hawthorn way
Scarlet satin, quilted seats,
Body of ebony.

Six black horses strain and pull
As though they served a load.
And no one ventures out that night
Upon that lonesome road.

No one is there to see it pass
Or wonder where it goes
With cracking whip to urge them on
To Heaven or Hell.....who knows?

Be well advised on Hallow's Eve
Within your house to bide
And do not dare to wander out
On Reehill's mountainside

For should you see upon the path,
It's told in tale and song,
This coach of finest ebony,
You will not live for long.

Your very soul will perish there
At such a cursed sight
And be stolen away for evermore
To endless, blackest night.

Jeanette Selfridge

Jeanette has always loved books. It wasn't, however, until after she suffered a nervous breakdown that she started writing. She was told to put her feelings down in a daily journal. From then on she started to write.

She has three children and two of them love books as much as she does. For Jeanette writing is therapy..

Butterflies Forever

Did you see the butterfly yesterday?
You marvelled at its beauty,
 Its array of colours ranging from lilac, pink and green.
I know you sensed me.
Your tears fell as you touched my photo.

You haven't just one photo, you have me everywhere.
As if you might forget me.
It's been over twenty long years.
Still, every day you think of me.

The pain is still there within.
You wish you could hold me again.
No chance to say goodbye
You were left broken.

I was only six when I died.
I had dark hair and freckles you loved.
My brown eyes shone whenever I saw you.
You treated me as a son.

It's not lonely up here.
Grandad Tommy John is up here too.
We are with you all the time.
We are in your heart, thoughts and the air you breathe.

So, Auntie Rose, listen for me.
I am in the wind that blows.
I'm that butterfly that you spy.
I'm that draft on your neck.

So hold on to your memories.
I'll never leave your heart.
You'll never stop loving me
I'll never stop loving you.

Life for you is hard now.
Your tears easily flow.
You survived losing me.
I know you'll survive this too.

Black Waters

It was a stormy night. The moon was full and had cast light up into the midnight sky and landscaped itself onto the face of the lake. The sky was illuminated with spots of pale blue right through to the darkest navy, and looked as if someone was standing shining a torch behind it.

A few yards from the water stood a clump of trees. These trees had years ingrained in the barks of their soul and many people had sat at their feet. Locally, these trees were known as the Witches' Arms and they even had their own legend. This legend was that people used to dump or drag things and leave them at the foot of these trees. Seemingly they had to hug the trees and ask for the trees to let them dispose of the item, or items, in the waters the trees faced. The ritual always had to be started at midnight and done under the light of a full moon. This ritual wasn't complete until you burnt a small fire in the midst of the trees. As the flames burnt, you asked for forgiveness for the sin just committed.

Then, as the fire burnt itself out, the item could be disposed of in the murky lake waters. Nothing ever came from the lake, things were only put in. The legend said that if someone took something from the water, that they would die a painful and harrowing death.

I was slumped by the clump of trees. To me they were just huge oak trees; I didn't know they were the Witches' Arms. I remember looking up at their branches. Two trees stood tall and their branches were mingling together as if grasping something. A fire was burning and I had disposed of the sin into the lake. Only a few moments had passed and for a while only my tears were the only thing moving. My tears quickly slithered on to the ground below. The leaves that were scattered under the trees had yet again got the tears of a sinner.

The victim of my sin was Charlie, poor, poor Charlie. His only sin was that he loved women. He liked them as different as mayo and chilli peppers. The only things Charlie looked for in women were a pulse and a different look from his last conquest. He loved them and left them. His biggest mistake was meeting me. He loved me, and then he left me. Big mistake. No one discards Hazel like a bit of unwanted meat. I can still recall the night he told me he was going.

"Babe, it's been great, but it just isn't working between us."

My heart was pumping furiously, like a pressure cooker about to burst its lid. How dare he! Well, right then and there I vowed no woman would ever bear the wrath of Charlie again. I had to be quick; the full moon was that night. I made him a last dinner. I laced it with a special seasoning of pills. He closed his eyelids to me for the last time. I soon got to work with the electric knife and scissors. I took off the arms first, then the legs. Lastly I removed the middle parts. I had worked quickly and the mess was greater than I expected. I licked my lips in the aftermath of my deed. I would never see Charlie smirk at me again.

The dismembered bits were gathered up and rolled in a carpet. The splash as the remains sunk into the waters, enthralled me. But after all my effort I was shattered and I decided to lie down by the trees.

My peaceful moment was disturbed by my mobile phone ringing. Suddenly my fears and emotions were raised to the highest pitch. I had forgotten to dump Charlie's phone! Now, somehow, his phone was ringing me!
I answered and I heard the booming voice of an irate Charlie. He had somehow woken up with a throbbing headache. He had no clothes on and whatever clothes he owned, had been destroyed. The only bits I had left him were the arms and legs of his favourite suit. Oh yes, and I left him a few gussets of his trousers; they might be needed to cover him up. He swore he would get me soon.

And I had placed up loads of mirrors in strategic positions. I had given Charlie a makeover. His head was shaven, along with his eyebrows and every bit of manly hair he was proud of. The scream I heard was obviously when he saw his face. I had carved 'Hazel' into his face - an everlasting reminder of me.

My last words to him were, "Hope you never forget me, babe, 'cos I'll never forget you, darling!"

Goodbye, Arthur

I have been with my Arthur, for over forty five years and he still makes me tingle, all over. Mostly my stomach churns, when he hands me his teeth with the remains of his dinner on them. He says I clean them better, the lazy sod. Crikey, men have an easy life you know.

When I met him, I thought he was God's gift to women. Now he is more like an oversized lump of lard. Gone is the wash board stomach. In its place are rolls and rolls of fat encased in a greasy skin. I dare say if I threw a dart at him he would burst and fly around the room like a deflating balloon. His head, too, is even shiny like a balloon.

He used to tell me I was the most beautiful woman alive. Now it is, "Don't sit there, that chair hasn't been reinforced!" Or he might make my day by saying, "Your arse is big enough without wearing that."

Our idea of a romance now is two fish suppers and falling asleep watching News at Ten. He used to take my breath away just by looking at him. Now he leaves me breathless by taking his shirt off. Well if you saw the size of his stomach it would make you gasp for air too.

I know you might be wondering why I am still with him. Well he is like the oldest, ugliest sofa you ever had, might not be much to look at, but it is cosy and comfortable. Anyhow, at seventy you don't want too many thrills. I know I couldn't leave him but the words 'till death us do part' seemed really alluring - he is worth more dead than alive!

I thought of stabbing him, but I hate gory things. Hitting him with a blunt instrument? Well, by the size of his head, it would take some whacking. So the only thing was to give him a fatal heart attack. At least then he would die of natural causes. I would have to seduce him. The last time I let Arthur near me was when we got drunk at our Rachel's wedding. He tried to throw me down on the bed like a wild animal and missed. I landed on the floor with a thud and was bed ridden for weeks. Arthur, on the other hand, had two black eyes. I might have done my back in but my fists still worked. Anyway the only swelling noticeable that night was his eyes.

My Arthur always liked silky negligees, black ones complete with black hold ups. He came that night from the pub bellowing.

"Woman dear, where is my food?"

I tried to put on my sexiest voice and said, "Never mind dinner, go straight to afters honey!"

He asked me what planet I was on, and as I never spoke he came looking for me. I draped myself seductively over the bed like a lioness seeking her lion. I started to wonder what was keeping him when I heard his voice.

"Where are you, woman?"

"In the bedroom. Come here."

"What is up now, woman dear?"

As he slowly opened the door I half propped myself up on the bed. His face peeked around the door"

As he said, "Crikey, Mildred!" his face started to redden and he started to swell in regions that he thought were extinct. My plan was slowly coming together. All he had to do was drop and I would be a merry widow.

I said nothing but purred slightly as he approached. His eyes were bulging and he was rubbing his hands. I moved up the bed and patted to the space beside me. Instead of lying beside me he leaped on top of me as if he was Spiderman. Now I was getting breathless, as his huge body lay there. I told him to be quick but he didn't move. There was movement but it was me!

Somehow I was standing looking down at Arthur. He was shaking something on the bed. I rubbed my eyes for a second. I was standing watching him shake a lifeless body. And he muttered the words, "Bloody Mildred, why, after all these years, do you get frisky?"

I watched as the doctor pronounced me dead. As the doctor said those words I saw tears fall down Arthur's cheeks as he moaned, "Not my Mildred! You might have been a nag, but you were my nag."

It turns out that just by chance Arthur had somehow smothered me with his huge stomach. As he leapt onto the bed he couldn't get his zip down. And as he lay there trying to undo his zip, I was being smothered.

I had somehow got *myself* killed!

My Girl

A golden ray of light shines upon your face, a golden curl falls loosely on your brow. Your green eyes sparkle. A smile breaks out on your sweet face.

The day you were born, a rainbow shone brightly. I was told you were special as soon as you were born. I'm proud of you my dear.

You'll never be a scholar You'll never read my poems You won't ever be literate You'll cry many a tear.

You might find it tough and say, "Why me?" I will get down at time. But I'll think of that rainbow and your smiling face.

My darling Shelley I know now why you're here. You're here to put that sparkle into our lives. Don't be someone you can't. I love you, faults and all.

None of us can do everything. So don't get upset. The road ahead might get rough. The only thing I am certain of is you. You're that bit of sunshine on a gloomy day. You're that added bit of fun. My life is so special because of you.

Gwen Tener

Gwen who is from Castlecaulfield has been involved with the Burnavon Writers Group, more or less, since it started. She has a part-time job and six grown-up children.

She writes short stories simply for pleasure and to get things out of her system.

She won first prize in the Dungannon Arts Festival Short Story Competition in 2008 and was runner up in 2009. She was also a finalist in the BBC My Story 2010 Competition.

Decisions

It was a last minute decision to go to the hairdresser's. The receptionist said at first that they weren't able to take her but then rang Donna back with an appointment for three o'clock. There'd been a cancellation. Everywhere the shops were closing early, staff wanted to get home. People were bustling and busy, full of Christmas cheer and secrets hidden in car-boots. Tonight the parcels and presents concealed in attics and under beds would be brought down for little children to find tomorrow.

But there was no Christmas Eve rush for Donna. It would be just herself and James again. Tomorrow they would have a bit of a lie in, the usual debate about going to the morning service - and the usual lies to each other that they didn't really fancy it, when they both knew that neither could face the infants lisping carols, the happy families spilling out of paper strewn cars, excited faces of children clutching new dolls and cars and computer games and sweets.

'You're sure about this, are you?' the hairdresser interrupted Donna's thoughts.

Donna nodded at her reflection and watched the knowing glint of the scissors as they began to cut. She had always said she would give it until she was forty. Tearing the page off the little tablet calendar this morning was like ripping off a sticking plaster; she had to brace herself, take a deep breath and pull in one swift sharp movement so that the pain hit her quickly and was over quickly.

And there it was - a big red 24 December 2008 - her fortieth Christmas Eve birthday.

'Your life is in your own hands – make sure you don't drop it,' the motto for today read.

In the mirror, she saw her long hair falling, helpless, useless, spreading over the white shiny tiles of the modern chrome and leather salon.

'My raven beauty,' James always called her, laughing at this pun.

'You're very brave going for such a drastic restyle,' the girl said to Donna's tense face in the mirror.

Donna looked at her. What age was she? About twenty? Twenty one maybe. What did she know about anything?

'It's my birthday. I thought I'd enter the new decade with a new style,' she said knowing that the girl would have no idea what she was talking about. The hairdresser began to tell Donna about someone she knew who had a birthday party in London and danced in the fountain in Trafalgar Square.

Donna tuned out of the conversation and re-focused on her own thoughts.

In the New Year, she would tell her manager that she could accept the overtime she had been offered. Now she could even take that job that meant travelling up and down the country. She had no ties. It was time she faced reality. Time she started to tell people that she wasn't going to have children – ever. James wouldn't mind if she had to attend the odd overnight conference. He might be glad not have to listen to her, to be free from seeing the disappointment in her face, feeling the twinge when a TV film has a scene with infants sleeping peacefully in cots or children swinging blithely in sunlit gardens.

'Are you sure you want spiky?' The scissors were paused in mid-air, shining viciously. Donna looked at the earnest eyes of the hairdresser and nodded numbly. If she spoke right now, she was afraid it would all spill out of her. All the pain and the longing and the fears and the waiting, all the hopes she had to let go.

On the floor, her dark locks would soon be swept into a bag and left out for the bin-men after the holidays. When she got home later, she would go to the room at the front of the house, the one that gets the morning sun, and take a black bag and put all the bootees and toys and the mobile with the teddies and the blankets - all the things that she had bought over the years and hidden from James. And she would take this bag and set it out too, for collection after the holidays. She wouldn't need these things after all. Turning forty meant abandoning the dream, turning forty meant recognizing reality, turning forty meant cutting her hair to face a new life.

The girl was rubbing gel through the tips of her cropped mane.

Donna hardly looked at herself and left the seat at the mirror to follow the girl to the desk, offering payment and a generous Christmas tip.

'Thank you. Happy Christmas.'

'Happy Christmas.'

Out of the salon into the mall, past shops full of tinsel and glitter and Santas and greenery, full of parents with children wearing multi-coloured bauble hats with matching mittens dangling from the arms of puffy anoraks, heading quickly for the draughty blackness of the exit, hoping no-one knew her because she needed to be home right now.

At the door of the Shopping Centre, the charity collector's tin rattled, like sharp stones on a tin roof. Donna saw the face of a little black child on the collection container looking helplessly at her.

Now she fumbled in her purse, taking out all the notes that were there and pushing them towards the surprised woman, who couldn't fit so many notes into her canister. Donna felt a half-plan forming in her head, so that she rushed to the car, and steered home as fast as she could. She went straight into the study, onto the internet looking for the site where they wanted volunteers for a school, an orphanage, a hospital, anywhere where she'd be able to have contact with little round faces that would look to her for help, for meals, for mothering.

And when he came home she told him that it was over and she would work her notice in the office and she was going to Africa to work with the poor children of Malawi. She had been speaking to some people and she had almost everything in her new life arranged.

And James listens to her intently and takes her in his arms and holds her and at last she is able to let go of the pain and she cries until his shirt is sodden and sticking to his skin.

Then he suggests that they try the IVF just one more time. They have the money and what use is it, if they can't try one more time?

And if this doesn't work, he says, he will come with her and they will work side by side with the needy, the hungry and the homeless.

He runs his hands over her shorn head and tells her that she is still his raven beauty and he would rather have his life with her, childless, than with any other woman. And slowly, she begins to smile and they sit beside the tree and he fishes out her birthday present. And she remembers the motto on the calendar this morning and realizes, that her life is actually in her husband's hands and more importantly that his life is in hers and they need to hold each other together for everything else to make sense. And, as she opens her present, she tells herself that forty is only a number, and the motto for tomorrow should be 'where there's life there's hope.' And maybe, just maybe, they might be able to face church tomorrow morning.

Fragile World; Perfect Globe

There was no splash. At least none that Iris heard. She hadn't even had time to scream. One minute she was standing on the cliff, the next, her foot must have caught in a root and she was plunging headlong, clean away from the rocks, towards the sea.

Everything went into slow-motion. Even as she was plummeting downwards, it was as if someone had put a finger in an old tape reel and slowed everything down. She was aware of the black rocks that embraced the cove, the pale blue eyes of the gannets, looking up momentarily from their nests on the shelving cliffs, the white headed waves whose roar grew louder.

Immersion was sudden, engulfing, like a pillow placed over her head and pushed into her ears. No splash. She must have sliced cleanly through the surface, like a diving bird, cutting through the deep green water. The surge of the ocean filled her head with noise. She opened her eyes, aware that the weight of water below her had already begun to slow her descent. White bubbles rose to the surface like exhaust fumes from a car. She looked up at the grey-white light that seemed to float on top of the water and wondered whether she would ever be able to get back there. Strangely, she felt no sense of panic.

She let herself fall; there seemed no point in resisting. Like a feather in a summer breeze, she was drifting slowly, inevitably, down to earth. She felt herself moving with the current, swaying like pond weed. The face of a boy with wild red hair and a flounce of freckles across his face, came into her head. She smiled to him in welcome. The taste of brine filled her mouth.

It's fitting that my life should end this way, she thought. In the end, everything comes full circle.

Her last words to Arthur had been sharp. "I'm fed up with you and your crazy ideas. Why can't you just enjoy your retirement like anyone else?" In her slowed-down, peaceful world, Iris could kick herself now. She should have made her final words to him more memorable. After all, they had had fifty four years together; it wasn't right that she was leaving him with such harsh criticism. He deserved a few kind words. He had been a good husband. She would have liked to have told him that much at least.

Recently, they seemed to be having so many arguments, especially since he joined that new environmental group, Green Shoots. He had retired from his job as a washing machine engineer about two years ago. Well, he was forced to retire; he hadn't really wanted to go. But no-one wanted washing machines repaired anymore. Everyone had to have a new model, the latest colour, the updated shape.

For a short time after, he had placed a small ad in the classifieds - 'I'll fix anything!' But even that kind of work dried up. No-one bothered mending things anymore.

"I don't know where it's all going to end." Arthur moaned, almost daily. "Rubbish doesn't just disintegrate, you know. Do they think the whole world is disposable?"

At first, Iris was glad that he had an interest, something to occupy him and keep him from under her feet. She sorted her waste into newspapers and tins and glass and stuff for compost bins. They didn't go on long flight holidays. She tried to buy organic foods and eco-friendly cleaning products.

But lately Arthur's views seemed to have become more strident. He lectured her about global warming, deforestation and alternative energies. He checked everything she bought, going through the grocery bags like a customs control officer, ranting if she bought something that he considered to be over-packaged or non-recyclable.

"Do you realize that the sea off the coast of Ireland is completely polluted?" he had asked her, only this morning over breakfast. She remembered how she had tried to look interested as she sipped her coffee and nodded. But, secretly, she wanted to tell him that he was an 'eco bore' and he should stop droning on. And just there now, a minute ago on the cliff top, he was explaining all about environmentally friendly pest control. She had switched off. She didn't want to listen to him. She never really listened to him. She could see that now.

She had only had one boyfriend before Arthur - Bobby McPherson, who lived two doors down from where she was born and who sat in her class at school and tried to copy her work. He had the most wonderful hazel eyes, with mischievous flecks of sunshine in them and he smelt of the outdoors and long summer days. She had met Arthur one night in the Odeon Cinema, when she and her friend, Mandy Hart, went to see *From Here to Eternity* for the second time.

Even now, after all these years, a blue vein stood out on Arthur's forehead if she ever mentioned her old boyfriend's name. He could never compete with Bobby, you see. All in all, however, Arthur had been a good husband and a good father. How sad that she wasn't going to get the chance to tell him now.

They had married in June. It was a lovely day, despite everything. Her mother wore a yellow linen suit with an embroidered neckline. She managed to look proud even through her tears. Her father refused to come to the wedding but, well, it was a different age then, wasn't it? After the wedding Arthur adopted Peter. It was plain that he wasn't Arthur's child, not with that distinctive red hair and those lovely hazel eyes. To be fair to Arthur, he never made a difference, even when the girls came along. Now that she had time to reflect on it - the difficulties in her marriage were not caused by her son. Now that she was looking at things this closely, she realized that it was, and had always been, Bobby McPherson who was the problem.

The wafting, floating feeling made her think of the long swaying grass in the meadow where she grew up and the dandelion clocks that she used to pick when she was a girl.

Please Mr Dandelion, can you tell me the time?

With her cheeks puffed out as big and round as gob stoppers, she blew until her lungs were empty.

One o'clock, two o'clock, three o'clock….

Her breath shattered the fragile perfect globe and the seeds dispersed into the wind, to be carried away by the breeze.

The meadow lay just at the end of the lane where she grew up. She and Mandy filled their days catching frogspawn and making stepping stones over the river that skirted the field, their dresses tucked into the elastic of their pants. The boys, Bobby McPherson and her brother, Johnny, were never far away. Sometimes they swung from the rope swing, further down the stream, yelling 'Tarzan' and whooping like Red Indians, or they fished with a piece of bamboo and some string with a bent pin on the end, frightening any potential catch with their laughter.

When they could persuade the boys to join in, they all played hopscotch together and Bobby would sometimes turn the rope for them to skip. She remembered the hedgerow along the lane, where the butterflies and bees partied all summer long. The ditch was an endless source of materials for their games – ladybirds, primroses, foxglove and honeysuckle. She could still remember the feeling of rain running off the bottom of her anorak, down her bare brown legs at the end of the summer and the metallic plop of blackberries as they covered the base of the pot.

They were happy days. Did the children nowadays have as much pleasure from their bubble-wrapped cardboard-boxed toys? Would future generations have the same childhood wonder in the beauty of the world? She was sorry now that she hadn't shared in Arthur's interest in the environment. Sorry that she had thought of him as an eco-bore. They had four grand-children and, her memory of those lovely days in the meadow made her realize that unless someone took a stand, those habitats for wildlife and flowers would all soon be gone. Arthur was right, you couldn't just spray everything with pesticides, killing micro-organisms that fed insects that in turn were food for the birds and other wildlife.

For the first time, Iris began to feel some pride in her husband's eco projects. It was, after all, an investment in the future of his children and grand-children. You couldn't leave the future to chance, blowing randomly like some fluffy dandelion seed carried in the wind, could you?

She looked around her and realized that she must have come to the bottom. Oil drums and pram frames and old shopping trolleys lay on the muddy sea floor. The current set her down gently on the sludge of the sea bed, and silt rose in a black syrupy cloud around her. She lay in the brown water, waiting for the sediment to settle. She hadn't realized the sea had become so dirty. Arthur was right. The world was fragile and we shouldn't just take it for granted.

Her cheek touched something slimy, and turning, she saw that it was a dead fish, shining bluish-purple, like a bad bruise in the sand. She moved away quickly and hit her elbow on the handlebars of an old bike. The sediment she had disturbed continued to settle like soot. This couldn't be her final resting place. This was nothing more than a rubbish tip. She should try to get back to Arthur and be more supportive of his projects in the future. She owed it to her grand-children. She would take them to the meadow and show them the dandelion clocks. She would teach them to care for their world.

She sat up and pushed her feet against the ground beneath her, cringing as the gloopy black mess sucked at her feet and reluctantly released them. She managed to get some upward momentum. She pushed her way through the disturbed debris, moving her arms in a swimming motion and beginning to kick her feet.

She had learned to swim in the fresh clear water of the lagoon, beyond the fields near her home. There, the fish were a healthy pink and brown and the silver water tasted of the mountainside and clean open skies. Bobby, Mandy her brother and Iris used to hold contests to see who could hold their breath longest under-water. Coming up to the long summer holidays, she and Mandy practised in the bathroom for weeks before challenging the boys. It became an annual summer ritual - who could stay under for longest. Bobby held the record of almost three and a half minutes by the time he was seventeen. That was why no-one really panicked, when he disappeared under-water for so long. They thought he had been at home practising in the bath, the way they all did. Johnny stood on the bank with his shiny new watch, counting the seconds, his voice rising with excitement when his friend passed five minutes. They all watched the rippled circle where Bobby had dived in, amazed at the endurance of his lungs.

By the time they decided that someone needed to take a look and by the time they got his feet unhooked from the weed in the pond, well, it was all too late wasn't it?

Her father carried him home. She walked behind them, her eyes fixed on her father's sodden trousers, clinging to his legs, dripping water the whole way into Mrs McPherson's living room, where he laid Bobby on the settee, as white and still as marble. The cry from Mrs McPherson seemed to rise slowly up her throat. She took the hem of her apron in both hands and pulled it up towards her mouth. But the wail escaped, loud and mournful, and her face crumpled, her head went back to open her throat wider, letting out the animal pain. Finally, her knees yielded and she sank slowly to the floor beside her boy on the settee. Iris leaned on the door frame sobbing, her hand cradling the base of her stomach.

She rose through the water now, heading for the grey light at the top. Would Arthur have summoned help by now? Would he be weeping on the cliff top? She did not know how he would manage without her, if she didn't make it. Perhaps he would go to the rallies with that Madge Ferrans with the nice hair, who always brought him an extra cake at the pensioners' club? The thought added extra strength to her swimming. She drove herself upward.

Her head emerged into the pale blue light, her mouth already open to draw in air in huge whooping gasps. She spat out the horrible dirty water and gulped in the clean clear air. It was a while before she noticed the silence which surrounded her. There was no sign of any rescue mission. No boat carrying frogmen buzzing around, looking for her. No helicopter, chattering overhead. No shouts from the cliff tops. Not even a police car. Just the caw of a few gulls overhead.

A piece of driftwood poked at her and Iris grasped it, hanging her arms and chest over it, as though she were drunk. She lay floating on the water, exhausted. She saw herself now, standing on the cliff top, looking out to the horizon, wishing that Arthur would stop rabbiting on about his pet subject. Why had Arthur not got help? Where was he? Was it her imagination or could she remember feeling the thrust of his open palms on her back, propelling her over the edge?

No-one was coming, that much was clear. The rhythmic slap of the waves was making her drowsy. Her head began to nod. She closed her eyes. He had been a good husband, that was true. But she had never really forgotten Bobby, had she? Arthur had probably guessed how it was many years ago. She couldn't understand why he had waited this long to do something about it.

In the distance, the burr of an engine made her look round. A boat was coming towards her like a great black fly. It cut the engine, just a few yards away and a man leaned towards her. Instinctively she reached out, looking into his friendly hazel eyes. The golden flecks of sunshine were still there, the red hair turned to white now but the skiff of freckles over his nose and cheeks unmistakable. Dreamily Iris inhaled the wonderful smell of outdoors and long summer days in the meadow. She slid gratefully off the driftwood, into his arms.

In this fragile perfect globe, she thought. Everything comes full circle in the end.

The Candle in the Wind

Sounds reached her consciousness first - the whisper of soft shoes on tiled floors, the murmur of voices somewhere in the distance, the intermittent drone of machinery of some kind – a heating system perhaps or a lift? Awareness grew in her that there was something strange happening.

Slowly Olivia opened her eyes. There was a long corridor of light to her side, electric light, not daylight and not the grey light that normally sifted from the street through the curtains of her bedroom, with the darker patch on the wall where the big mahogany wardrobe stood.

She could see the dark shapes of beds in the ward now and could hear the sleeping noises of other people beside her. Hospital. She must be in hospital. She called out but her voice couldn't seem to form words. With some effort, she made a primitive cry, like a cat separated from its young.

The whispering shoes came quickly to her bedside. The nurse's face loomed close. Olivia tried to ask what happened but instead the moaning noise came out again.

'There, there, Mrs Scott. You're all right. You're in St Matthews'. You've had a wee stroke.'

The nurse checked her temperature and took her pulse. From her pillow, the patient could see the hand held by the nurse was old. There were great hollows between the sinews leading to each finger and the knuckles were deeply lined and knobbly. It looked like her mother's hand, Olivia thought. And yet it must be hers.

Again she tried to ask, and again an unrecognizable sound emitted. It was as though her tongue had been removed or her jaws weren't working.

'Ssh,' said the nurse again, her voice as soft as a soothing hand on her forehead. 'Sssh, now. We'll check you out in the morning. Go back to sleep.'

Olivia felt her lids dragged down by the weight of the information she had been given. When had she got so old? When did she get to be old enough to have a stroke? She heard the swish of the nurse's turn on the floor.

She saw herself as she used to be - the tilt of her head, the arch of her back, the curve of her calf - everything about her was toned and fit. She was a ballerina, she had made people weep with her performances; she couldn't be old enough to have a stroke.

Her first leading part was when she was 24. In the hush of expectation, centre-stage, alone in the halo made by the spotlight on the darkened stage, she stood on the points of her toes, her arms extended high above her head, like a flame of a candle on a still August night. For a moment, it seemed as if all the air had been sucked out of the auditorium. And then, the music started. The flame began to move, flickering to the left and right, stretching straight and tall, reaching low, darting here and there. She moved, she spun, she lit up the stage. She was the music, she was the dance, she was the candle in the wind.

In her hospital bed, Olivia inhaled deeply. She heard again the final thrum of the orchestral violins, the pin-drop silence as her performance ended, the roaring swell of gathering applause. She felt again the weight of the bouquet in her arms, the rush of emotion filling her chest, the tingle of tears at the back of her eyes. She walked to the front of the stage, bowing low. The applause grew until it completely filled her ears. She exhaled noisily and the flame burned no more.

A Wee Easy Tea

It was the smell from the home bakery that did it. As familiar as a caress, a hug from your granny, the aroma enveloped me, pulling me towards the golden loaves and shiny pastries sitting tantalizingly on the shelves. A vision of a wheaten bread and ham tea came into my head. Lettuce and tomatoes and hard boiled eggs. A wee easy tea, I would have called it when they were all at home. A rest from cooking for one night.

Nowadays my elbows go red from sitting at my old pine kitchen table, reading magazines. It's only me and him and sometimes only me now. The farm keeps him busy you see. He doesn't always come in for a meal. Says the house is too quiet without the children.

I've got so much freedom now. The children have all left and I.. well.. look at the work it saves me. I don't have one quarter of the washing. Four boys and two girls – that's a lot of washing. One an engineer and one a motor mechanic - well you can imagine. And I don't have the problem of finding places to get the darn things dry either. We don't even need a tumble dryer anymore. The old one is just sitting in the garage, like a great white Christmas present that didn't suit.

And the potatoes. Imagine peeling potatoes for five men every day of the week. Thank goodness for frozen chips. They were a life saver when they were all going through that great eating spurt that boys go through. You know when they could eat six slices of bread and six spuds and still look for extra custard and tart. I don't miss the cooking that's for sure.

And the traipse of girls that came through my door before they were done. Tall, small, fat, thin, blonde, brunette - you name it – they were brought home by one of my boys. I've had my day of sitting through teenage DVDs while they sat with arms round awkward gawks of girls whose bony elbows could have cut bread.

And now they're gone.

Tim didn't come home at all last summer. Or maybe, now that I think about it, he stayed a week in August – between trips and even then he was out every night. Catching up with his friends he said. Then he went to America to help out in some under-privileged children's camp.

James is married and just lives down the road but he has two children now and his wife likes him to come home straight after work. We've had that one out. No calling in – just straight home. She needs him to help with the children. And she makes her family Sunday dinner, so they can't come here and they haven't enough room for us there.

Johnny is working in a bar in Cannes at the moment. That's in France and you don't pronounce the 's'. He wants to live in France for a while to improve his French before settling down with a job teaching languages. He didn't get the jobs he applied for and what was there to hold him here anyway? That Alexis Drummond has a lot to answer for. I'm glad he doesn't have to see her every day in the village. Flaunting herself like that. I closed my eyes at her mother the other day. She looked as if butter wouldn't melt but I wanted to let her know that she didn't fool me.

Anyway, where was I? Oh yes, the children and a wheaten bannock. John is at the ploughing and he won't stop for a cooked meal, so a nice wee bit of ham and wheaten will be just lovely. Did I tell you there's only the two of us now? Grace and Sharon, the two older girls, well they're both married and away a long time. Sharon's in Belfast. She visits when she can but she has three children at that age. You know when they roll their eyes and they can't lift their feet when they walk? Sometimes when she comes with the trio in tow, I just want to tell her to pack them all back into the car and go home. If they can't be civil to their grand-mother... I don't know what way she's rearing them. I really don't.

Grace lives close by, but her husband – well he seems to come and go and she tries to hide it from me. I've offered to help but she doesn't want me interfering. Interfering! Me! And if she fell down in the street and I held out my hand to help her up, would that be interfering too?

The floury sweet smell of McDermott's Home Bakery hasn't changed. It must be two or three years since I was last here. Not since Tim, the youngest left home. Yes, she says she'll split a bannock. Well we'll never eat a whole one between us.

Beautiful, the wheaten was absolutely beautiful. The crumbs are all over the table. There's another job, I don't miss. Dishes for eight people and then the floor having to be swept every mealtime otherwise the crumbs and food scraps would get tramped into the good carpet. Nowadays the floor stays clean from one meal to the next.

I do crosswords and keep the garden tidy and I meet Hazel for coffee every Wednesday and sometimes a walk but you know sometimes I come home to my lovely clean house and I wish... I wish.... There's just this hole and I can't seem to fill it. I remember the way it was when I used to come home from work and the dirty breakfast dishes were sitting in the sink with the cornflakes hardened to the sides, because no-one could be bothered to turn the tap on. And sometimes I wish, as I look around my beautiful home and I remember the way I had to scold about how hard it was to keep things tidy. And sometimes I just wish. I just wish….

There's the phone. I leave the crumby table and lift the receiver. Wrong number. The receiver clicks back hollowly onto the cradle, loud in the empty house. I survey our tea table and lean my whole arm, right down to my wrist and the side of my hand across the cloth and swipe the crumbs onto the floor. Then I stand and wipe the crumbs sticking into my skin onto the floor. At least tonight, when I come home from Hazel's, I will have to sigh and roll up my sleeves and brush the floor, muttering about the state people have left the place in.

Rachel Wardle

Rachel is a part time teacher and full time mum to two beautiful children. She lives in an idyllic place with a very understanding husband. She loves reading and has an eclectic taste in authors and genres.

Rachel would like to write a book and, who knows, she may yet do so!

Due to a transcript error the story Entitled *Big Expectations* has been wrongly attributed to Rachel Wardle. Unfortunately, because of this, Rachel has been under-represented in this publication. We apologise for this mistake to Rachel and to you the reader. We hope this does not mar your enjoyment of this excellent book.

Big Expectations

"Don't you say anything." He knew by her tone that she meant it.

As they entered, he wondered were there shades of paint that were only manufactured for hospitals. The corridor walls were hospital off-white. The doors were all different colours – reds, blues, greens, oranges. It looked like an interior designer's nightmare.

They sat silently in the waiting area. Tina picked her way through an "OK" magazine that had been left lying on the tables for the patients. He briefly wondered why they never leave out magazines suitable for male readers. Aren't men patients too?

He remembered his delight when Tina told him she was pregnant. He'd hugged her and kissed her. They'd laughed.

"We'll have to give it a temporary name," said Tina.

Once, he'd read that a baby is the size of a normal full-stop when it is conceived. So he'd named it their Full-Stop.

The midwife swept the scanner over Tina's jellied belly. A triangular structure focussed on the screen, jumping slightly right, then left as the midwife worked. Finally part of the image disappeared and reappeared rhythmically.

She turned and smiled. "That's your baby's heartbeat."

They smiled back. They'd asked for the baby's sex not to be identified and the midwife had been careful to only refer to "it". She made tiny adjustments, froze the screen and pressed the print button.

"Everything's fine," she said.

Tina watched, eyes bulging in fascination.

"What size is it now?" He'd wanted to ask that. Tina had said that he'd only ask something stupid, that they'd think he was an eejit and that it would be embarrassing when they would come back for the next scan. So he stayed silent. It wasn't easy.

"About the size of a thumb." He would have asked, "Whose thumb?" Thumbs come in different sizes. Didn't the midwife know that? His thumb was twice the size of Tina's. These things were important. He stayed quiet.

Rachel Wardle **149**

"Thanks for not asking questions," said Tina in the car on the way home.

"Sure, you know me. I'd only make an eejit of myself." She laughed, leant over and kissed him on the cheek.

"Thanks" she said again.

It was round about then that his life was turned upside down. Tina went public and told all her friends. All hell broke loose. Suddenly their house was full of women. Sisters, friends, work colleagues, aunts. Sometimes men would be dragged along. They'd just shake his hand and say congratulations. Job done.

The ladies gave Tina a hug. The questions would begin. "How old is it?" "How long have you known?" "Have you been sick yet?"

He just let them get on with it. Job done.

Then Tina went mad. A room in the house would have to be decorated immediately. He'd wanted to do things the old way. It was always thought unlucky to get things ready in advance of the new baby. The Gods would punish those who expected too early. She was unconvinced, describing the old ways as "a load of old nonsense".

He moved the furniture out of Full-Stop's new room without complaining. She studied the Dulux colour chart.

"What do you think of that colour?" she asked, pointing out a warm pastel shade.

"Can't we wait to see what colour Full-Stop likes?" he'd answered.

"For a moment, I thought you were serious." she said, laughing. "And you wonder why I stopped you asking questions in the hospital?"

"You choose" he said.

He just got on with the painting. The women kept coming. More questions.

"Can you feel it kicking yet?" Hands were placed on Tina's belly and squeals of delight issued when kicks were felt.

"Do you mind if I ask something?" He stopped on his way into the utility room for a paintbrush.

They turned and looked at him.

"Which foot does it kick with?" They looked at him like he was an eejit. Leaning back so that the others wouldn't see, Tina giggled quietly before composing herself.

Returning with the paintbrush, he stopped again.

"It's just that I want to know whether to play him at the top of the right or top of the left." He kept his face straight

"Right" said Tina.

Without replying, he continued upstairs. It was no bother to him to keep his face straight. He was always amazed by what people believed once they think they're smarter than you.

When they'd gone, Tina came upstairs and thumped him on the arm.

"I nearly burst. You and your bloody football. What if it's a girl?"

"I'll still play her top of the left. You can't make a difference."

She thumped him again. They laughed together as they always had. She loved his craziness, seeing it for what it was – a gift. He had the ability to say the wrong thing at the right time and she loved it. Her friends would never understand. They just saw it as craziness, not seeing that he only did it to stun people into silence or laughter. He was equally happy with either result.

She enjoyed telling him what had happened after he'd left the sitting room. They giggled uncontrollably when she told him that Rhonda had asked her was he serious. Rhonda was very intelligent. She'd never see. He collapsed with laughter when Tina said that she'd told Rhonda that he was. He kissed her affectionately and said, "Well done!"

In the weeks that followed, Full-Stop bulged Tina's belly and slowly took over their lives. He, she or it had to be considered at all times. Phone calls made. Worries calmed. Preparations made. And then the women started to buy things for Full-Stop. Rattles. Blankets. Changing mats. Baby boxes. The men just stood about. He brought them into the kitchen and they talked the usual nonsense. Full-Stop's room was finished. Job done.

Tina started to buy things too. Steriliser. Cot. Seats. He just fetched and carried and piled the stuff into another bedroom. Full-Stop was aptly named as he was putting an end to normal life as they knew it.

"Would you mind bringing the stuff in?" she asked when she returned from her latest shopping trip. Off he went. No need to answer. It'd have to be done now. The back of the car was jammed full of nappies. He made four trips, piling the nappies on the sofa. Tina busied herself checking everything.

"Can I ask something?"

She recognised the worry in his voice and looked up. He waited.

"Well?" she said.

"I've never seen so many nappies in my life. Are we expecting a baby elephant?"

"Behave," she said. "You had me worried there for a moment."

"I know," he said. He knew that she knew that this was all strange to him, that he'd never really thought about it. But they'd be fine. She loved his craziness. As she patted her belly, she hoped that Full-Stop had inherited that craziness too.

Just Leave It

"Just leave it."
Just leave it? I can't just leave it. But she won't let me talk, not now. The shutters are up. She'll be polite for the rest of the evening; will speak to me like a ghost.
"Would you like a cup of tea? Something to eat, perhaps?"

All the time I can feel her anger simmering beneath the surface. We'll sit in separate rooms. She'll read and I'll watch TV. Even if she wants to watch what I am watching, she won't – a point of honour. The deliberate distancing. Her book will be a shield, preventing the catch of the eye, stopping any attempt to start a conversation to try and resolve our problem.

"No," she said, "just leave it!"

God, I wish I could, but words said and unsaid are jumbling in my head. I take in her cup of tea. She has to put the book down to take it and the biscuit. I grab my chance.

"I didn't mean it, the way I said it."
She purses her lips.
"Really?"

God, I hate that sarcastic tone. I try to keep a handle on my temper.
"Yes, really. You know I'm not like you. I find it difficult to express myself the way you do." She shrugs. She's not giving an inch.

Is there any point? Should I just leave it? Take her at her word and have her sulking all night and the cold shoulder at bed time? Never go to sleep on an argument, my dad always said, but I'm sick and tired of this.

Really just want to leave it, just this once. But I can't.

"Look, we need to talk," I say.
She sighs and gives me that 'all right, I'll humour you' half smile.
"Talk then," she says.
"I do like your family but your sister is a bitch. She has always been jealous of you, of us. She puts you down. She is nasty on purpose. I love you. I hate to see you like this. I do not have, nor have I ever had, any interest in her. It is all in her head. How could you possibly think I could fancy her chicken legs? You are all I want; all I have ever wanted."

I watch her melt, the tension fade away.

"You really piss me off," she says with the laugh clear in her voice.
"I know," I say, "And I'm glad."

I'm glad that I didn't just leave it. No, I'll never do that. I love her, you see.

My Treasure Box

In my box you will find:
A soft kiss,
A calloused hand,
A huggle
And a smile.

Rich velvet,
Melting chocolate,
A glass of wine
And a roaring fire.

A family meal,
Crisp new pages,
Clear blue winter sky
And comfort in the dark of night.

It's in His Kiss

It's not the how but the why. After forty six years of marriage you'd think everything would be fine. Thank goodness that nice young police constable lived next to me.

I knocked on his door and he came quickly enough, not quite masking his exasperation at being disturbed on his evening off. He mustered his manners and invited me in. Well, I told him straight. Henry is dead and I need you to see him now. He soon became very professional as he walked me back to my house. Henry had that funny grey look that indicates lifelessness and one glance at him was enough to set the wheels in motion. I suppose I could have told him there and then but he was too busy enjoying himself, reporting it in, securing the scene, all the things I so enjoy on C.S.I. on Channel 5. They took Henry away and left me in the care of a nice police girl; I suppose I shouldn't call her a girl but I never quite got round the idea of girls being policemen; well you know what I mean.

Things were different when they returned. Obviously the autopsy results were back. I was escorted down to the police station, to Interview Room One in fact. Rights read, tape recorder on; it was all very exciting.

The detective was very serious; still he was young enough to be my son. Though God hadn't seen fit to bless us with children. There was a lot of humming and hawing but the upshot was Henry had been poisoned. The detective dramatically paused at this, I don't know why; it wasn't news to me. Apparently there had been enough heart medicine in his system to fell a horse and it was the same heart medicine I had been prescribed.

I didn't quite roll my eyes though the temptation was there. "Yes, I know," I said. After all I did spend a good half an hour with my pestle and mortar and me with my arthritis and all. I mixed it in with his favourite stew, he didn't notice a thing.

So, eventually, he got round to the real question. As I said at the start "It's not the how it's the why." Well, forty six years of marriage and that TOAD decided he could kiss Maisie Abernathy. Well, he won't be doing it again. Will he?

Relaxation is for the Birds

I understand the concept of relaxation, but find the practice of it a guilt ridden process. I love to read, that's how I relax, but I don't read gently. I devour books. I speed read. If I like an author I will read everything she or he has written. It's addiction, not relaxation.

I like cooking, entertaining. Having dinner parties is somewhat curtailed now that I have small children but in any case the build up, the preparation and the actual night are hardly relaxing.

I like massages, pampering, days out with my mum or my best friend, Brenda. But my mind doesn't respond well even while my muscles are unwinding under expert touches. I'm thinking, making lists in my head – not the desired response!

I enjoy my children. I delight in their new discoveries and marvel that they are mine. But I worry all the time about their health and well-being. I keep them to a pretty rigid schedule so no, they are not relaxing either!

I don't even switch off in books or films; I become emotionally involved. My husband looks askance. "You're not crying again, are you?"
"I can't help it; it's so sad/so wonderful/so whatever." – but never 'so relaxing'!

People go walking to relax; I don't. I walk, if I have to, to get somewhere; not just to walk – it's not my idea of relaxation.

I prefer silence to music. I can't sing or draw. Paintings don't inspire me. I find it difficult to switch off. Even while driving to work I'm planning out my lessons in my head.

The idea of curling up with a good book, a glass of wine and some chocolate in front of a roaring fire sounds idyllic, but in reality I polish off the wine and chocolate, stoke up the fire and get down to the really serious business of reading my book as quickly as possible.

As he's from Manchester my husband refers to women as birds. Well this bird will have to disagree with the saying that 'relaxation is for the birds'. Maybe, but not for this one!

Alan Wilson

Alan developed his interest in writing when he became a father.
In our lives story plays a large part: from fairy tales to true life; drama to war.

He feels he is on an ever important search for truth through the books of prophets. "The most important aspect of a story," he says, "is to learn we are not alone, and this is a great gift to pass on to our children and to each other."

Alan writes in a variety of forms and has had work published in local papers.

Moving Day

Brian had been dreading this day. Ever since he had learnt his father got a new job in the city his heart had sunk. A great opportunity for his father maybe, but Brian has been feeling the strain of 'upping roots' for this past few weeks. At first was the welcome excitement of all the attention he got, but after came the realisation that he would not see his friends every day. Being the 'new kid' would set in and that wasn't so appealing. So the initial buzz didn't last, as the excitement was soon replaced with a sickly feeling of worry. For it is tough enough to be a small, skinny twelve year old in a town school. "I'll be eaten alive," he thinks to himself, imagining what things will be like at St. John's, a school with well over fourteen hundred pupils. "Maybe I'll be lucky and not be noticed. Naw, that'll be worse," he continues to argue with himself as his mum shouts from down the stairs, breaking the train of thought.

"I'm in my room. What is it?"

"John's here."

"Well, send him up then," he barks the order in annoyance as he makes his way to the bathroom to wash his face in an attempt to disguise any sign of crying.

"Where you at?" John half shouts.

"Over here, what's up lad?"

"Not much," John replies, looking up from the floor, "What's wrong? Are you crying?"

"Naw, lad, I was loadin' up the van and I got dirty," he replies, trying to make it sound like it is the only obvious reason.

"Aww right, it's just you're all red."

"Am I? Must be the soap."

"We're havin' a match round the back, lad. We're all lookin' you out. What do you say?" Brian has a look on his face now of complete relief.

"Good job you landed, John," he says excitedly, for he has nearly forgotten to say his final goodbyes. Not that he is happy about leaving everyone behind, far from it, but he is getting away from the coldness his home has now become.

"Ma!" shouts Brian as the boys walk down the stairs and enter the kitchen.

"What?" Trea asks, stopping her conversation with her friend Joyce.

"I'm off to say 'bye to everyone, I'll be back in an minute." Trea looks over and sees a nervous, heartbroken, angry child that the excitement can't hide. She'd like to shake a smile on his face but simply replies softly, "Ok, love I'll send your Dad for you when we're ready." The boys walk off without saying another word until they reach the gate, then talk of who all is there and whose ball is being used takes over until they reach the green behind the estate.

"Thanks for making the coffee and bringing everything around. I don't know what I was doing packing ours away. I mean, it could have sat in the front of the van."

"Think nothing of it, happy to help. Have you been talking with anyone in Belfast today?" asks Joyce refilling the pot.

"I got talking with Mrs. Wood, mind the neighbour opposite I told you about?"

"Oh yeah, the nosey one."

"Yes, handy to know for now. She rang to say the first van load had arrived."

"That was nice of her. Suppose it's all coming together now," Joyce says with a quick half hearted smile.

"I'll be glad when we're all settled in. It's going to take Brian a long time all the same."

Trea begins to wrestle with an idea of staying. "It will be harder for him to adjust that's part and parcel with this, you know that," she said with a hardened look, handing Joyce a filled mug. "Well, it's that age where nothing's right. He thinks the world is ending."

"Give him time. He'll soon know it's for the best."

"I just wish he could see that now."

"Trea, where's your head at? He's thinking about all his friends here."

"And don't I know that!" she replies, now in deep thought, holding her mug in both hands close to her mouth, gazing out the window.
Soon an hour passes without the children really noticing it.

"Well that's one thing we won't miss," Peter shouts jokingly, buckled over and holding his face.

"Sorry about that, lad, but if you hadn't kicked it so hard I would have been able to catch it. Look how red my knee is!"

"You're well used to it by now."

"Aye, and you'd think you would be too!" Brian replies getting one up on Peter.

"There's your Da, lad."

Brian looks up and sees his father walking towards him, "The last is loaded son, we'll be heading off soon."

"Alright, Dad," he says with a nod of the head. His voice stiffens as the small group of boys and girls gather around him.

"Here lad we got you this," Gary hands him a Derry G.A.A cap, "Just in case you start thinking you're an Antrim man now."

After a quick laugh and a few cheeky remarks Brian inspects the cap. "And you've all signed this?" he asks after reading all the Good Luck wishes scribbled on it.

"Yeah, just finished it before you came around," Peter answers and another friend adds, "We'll miss ya, lad." Everyone joins in. Remembering something, Brian asks for the marker and then the hugs and handshakes are exchanged and all move off, leaving Brian and Mary-Kate still hugging.

"I wish we were older. This isn't fair," she whispers.

"I know, I'll miss you the most." The hug tightens. "I gave you my new number, didn't I?" He feels her nodding her head, which is pressed against his shoulder. "And I'll ring you tomorrow."

"Brian!" his father shouts.

"I gotta go. Bye-bye."

They push away. Mary-Kate joins her friends and Brian runs off in the opposite direction, clutching the hat and marker, far in front of his father, rushing to number thirteen as fast as his legs can carry him. His head starts to hurt as it overloads with every memory of good times, hardship, his first fights and medals, the fun games, his first album, posters, all that defined his identity. And the embarrassing times when he was caught playing tea parties with Mary-Kate! "I've got to let them know I was the first there, it's more than walls,' he thinks. He charges into the kitchen, past a shocked looking mother, who is left calling after him. Without response or stopping he stomps up the stairs, his feet sending an echo around the empty house off the bare floor boards.

It's so small looking with everything gone, already not feeling like home. He reaches his room, the emptiness of the house reflecting how he feels toward the new house. Quickly he opens the door to the built-in wardrobe, drops to his knees choking back more tears, and starts to write his statement on the inside wall, 'Who ever shall have this room after me, remember I was here first and it will always be mine.' He finishes off with his signature. It looks impressive in bold black letters.

He now feels calm, with some sort of claim to the room. It gives him hope of getting back some day to claim his home again.

"Brian, come on!" shouts his mother. "What are you doing? We're in the van."

"Right, Ma, just finishing up. On my way now."

He walks off toward the front door with a comfortable smile of hope that the next child will take to the room as he did. For it has been more than just walls for him, it's been his haven from all trouble, his sanctuary within a home, where he first learned of music, where the homework was done and where friends stayed over.

If the young lad could take his bedroom with him, he would, for then it wouldn't be as if he's leaving everyone behind. And that feeling of safety Brain had become accustomed to would not be leaving him.

In the van, with his father behind the wheel and his mother to his right, he sits quietly. His father revs the engine.

"We all ready?" asks his father.

With a quick, "Aye," from his mother, Brain adds, "Suppose! Let's go and see what's so great about the new place."

"You'll see, son, you'll see."

Likeness

She is a lot like me. Nothing could stop her. Every day she'd be looking to see what she could make out of stone, glass, clay or fabric. Her first project, I remember, was making a little something out of the little shells she had gathered on the coastline of Coarfunic. After the picnic she walked around on her own, not wanting any help, and gathered as much as she could in her favourite plastic beaker. We had called to her a few times but, as I would have done at her age, she simply called back, "I'm all right."
The next we heard of her she had returned with the beaker filled to the brim with all sorts of shells – clams shells, empty snail shells – along with smooth stones with holes in them. She knew what she was going to do with them. She was so excited, smiling away, but, as I would have done, would say nothing until it was all done – in case something would happen.

But what was the first thing she made?

Oh yes, I was getting to that. Do you see the shiny necklace around my wife's neck? Well, she spent weeks on those stones and shells, polishing, protecting, covering them with nail polish. All for her Mum's birthday.

What age was she then?

Eight years old, so if your wee one is showing interest now, let her be and she'll find her way.

You and your wife must be so proud.

I didn't ever think we'd be standing in her own studio. But look how happy my wife is. I think our girl didn't do it only for herself, but also for her Mum. Like me, she'd do all to find her way in life and keep her mother smiling.

Old Hope with Seasons Greetings

"Hi, Snake! Snake!" Jonny half shouts while shaking Snake out of his sleep. "Wake up Snake! The line across the street is forming. Waken up!!"

"Aye, I'm awake, alright, I'm awake!" replies Snake as Jonny keeps badgering him.

The two men dust themselves down with a half hazy head between them, thanks to the cheap wine from the night before. "How do we look?"

"We'll be alright after a wash and a bite to eat" replies Jonny. "Today should be a good day, what do you think?"

"Just you hang on to that bag of yours and I'll hang on to mine. After this clean up and dinner we'll have a Merry Christmas" says Snake as the two men walk across the street to the soup kitchen.

"You're right, lad, we'll give the others the gifts after the shower."

"As always," says Snake and they take their places in the queue. Talking with others about the begging game nothing but lies are told, for to tell of any success would end with a mugging. These two buddies are old hands on the homeless scene having been on the streets for twenty years. They met over thirty years ago in a roadside diner waiting for a connecting coach. As naive teenagers on their way to the city to make their fortune they made friends instantly. Jonny had been calling Bruce Snake since then and rarely ever called him by his real name.

Today the soup kitchen will be transformed into a banquet hall, as a turkey dinner will be had by many. Now with nearly a hundred people gathered, along with a few stray cats and dogs, Jayne opens the doors. It doesn't take long for the kitchen to fill, over flowing with bodies all hungry. Volunteer workers rush about, most of them seasonal, for the soup kitchen is always busier in the winter, especially on Christmas Day.

As the two enter the main hall Snake catches sight of Jayne, their friend, who gives them the nod to go on up to her room. Every Christmas Jayne lets her friends use the shower in her apartment; it's her gift to them. It's a small three roomed dwelling which is in the same building as the soup kitchen, all run by the Salvation Army. It allows her friends to have some privacy away from all the commotion and gives her some company when she stops for dinner. She too had landed in the big city with big dreams of fortune, fame and marriage. All were shattered soon after landing and Jayne had lived with Jonny and Snake on the streets. But she had got

herself this small position a few years back and took it when she could. The three friends knew that this was a great position and would not do anything to disrupt that, for Jayne was lucky to be there and she knew it.

After getting cleaned up, Snake and Jonny exchanged their gifts. The gifts are made up of clothes and boots got from the Salvation Army Second Hand Store, except for Jayne's. They are brand new. This year it's a set of bath towels and the ever predictable box of chocolates, the ones she loves so well. Each could have got his own clothes, but there was more of a Christmassy feel in doing things like this.

"These boots are some job, but they're two sizes too big," laughs Jonny, lifting one foot and keeping his bent knee.

"Well," says Snake, "You know what they say about men with big boots?"

"What?" Jonny says loudly.

"They need big feet to fill them!!" he exclaims, laughing cheerfully. "Put them other socks on, what are you going to do with them if you don't?"

"Well, I was going to, I mean with.." he pauses "I don't know. I wasn't thinking."

The men have a laugh, a loud healthy one, the kind that sets a mood of joy that lasts for the rest of the day. They pass the next few hours watching the television and finishing a crossword in an old newspaper, until Jayne appears with the dinner.

Jonny answers the door, with Snake standing behind him.

"Merry Christmas!" shouts Jayne as she pushes in the tea trolley.

"Merry Christmas! You're a star!" the men reply.

"That's not all. Look!" says Jayne, pulling a tea cloth from the bottom shelf.

"Double helpings of sherry trifle." an excited Jayne says.

"Brilliant! Will they not be missed?" asks Snake.

"Not at all. I made them especially for us."

"You're a true trooper, Jayne" says Snake. "Now let's get stuck in."

The three friends sit at the dinner table and eat their banquet, talking over the events of the past week. Jayne had been startled about the news of a mutual friend, Billy the Bones, who had passed away during the month. After the meal, Jayne, still feeling a bit upset, gets her presents. She smiles again and the traditional Christmas night celebrations begin. This consists of three good friends and two special bags.

"Well, Jonny, what are we smoking tonight?" asks Snake.

"Marlboro. What's wetting the mouth?" and he pulls out five fat packs from his bag and sets them on the table.

"Wild Turkey!!" exclaims Snake, revealing two bottles in his brown paper bag.

"Towels, chocolates and good company. You guys can still show a woman a good time, I'll get the glasses."

These friends will forget the troubles of the outside world, if only for one night. They will reminisce on the days all three were together with others that are no longer there, for the streets claim many lives most people never hear about, although their friends do. The talk continues of the dreams they all shared and of past conquests that were embarked upon with whole hearted enthusiasm, only to be met with failure and disappointment. How naive and stupid they must have looked! Now they share a laugh to compensate for the dreams of fame and fortune which never materialised. As time passed these dreams had been down sized somewhat, from the thoughts of fortune chasing to just trying to get through until the next day. The obstacles they experienced in street life, and the feeling of life not ever changing, had set in long ago and kept the men on the corner. Jayne had got sick of that, and took on the challenge of getting on with things, while all the while telling the other two, to do the same.

After singing into the small hours, the men decide to leave, for Jayne has gotten very emotional and appreciative for all life has given her lately and has gone on to plague the two with her hopes for them but they're too stubborn to listen to anything other than sympathy.

"If you're not going to stay, at least head to the shelter. I've asked Berenice to keep a room for the both of you," Jayne says with a trembling voice, for this can be taken the wrong road.

"I'm not sure," says Snake as Jonny adds, "Sure if it doesn't work out, we'll lose the corner outside."

But this only annoys Jayne. "For God's sakes, I've gone to a lot of trouble getting a dishing gig for you pair!!!!"

"What do think you're at?"

"Who said you could do that?"

This is the response Jayne was dreading - anger.

"I got you a job at Yang's restaurant. It was meant to be a job from the shelter but....look if you want the corner go out and get it. Just remember your misery will always be out there. It's your happiness that will pass."

She hugs her friends with a different air and says nothing as they leave. Tearful now, she heads off to bed while Jonny and Snake go for a walk to talk over their options, not that there are many, but an issue like no drink every day would be a big step, especially when the begging game paid so well for it. But their love for a friend who went to all that trouble outweighs all else.

As hope of reality changing sets in, they lie in a warm room with a soft bed and clean sheets each. With words like: 'It's not going to be easy.' and 'Maybe it'll be different this time.' being exchanged across the room, a sense of accepting the change took over their thoughts.

Gift from God

I remember long days of kicking ball and playing soldiers. Without a care in the world we would climb trees, walk rivers, fight and forget.

I wish things were like that all the time.

But not in this life! The leaves will fall and rivers flow and as we get older the games change.

Now you're here and the endless days are yours. I worry now so you don't have to. If there's anything from my childhood I can give you it's this. Just you run on without a care, and enjoy life.

We have our whole lives to learn. Friends will come and go. So play, laugh, love and forgive quickly for time is precious and we don't have long.

Live your life to be happy

For what made me the man I am today I wouldn't wish on anybody. But God won't give us anything we can't handle.

In case you need a helping hand, remember I'm here and I'll do what I can to protect you.

For life is good - but better when you're here with me.